# Also by Gary Paulsen

*Murphy's Herd*
*Murphy's Gold*
*Murphy*

# MURPHY'S STAND

## Gary Paulsen
## and
## Brian Burks

Walker and Company
New York

First published in the United States of America in 1993 by Walker
Publishing Company, Inc.

Published simultaneously in Canada by Thomas Allen & Son Canada,
Limited, Markham, Ontario

Library of Congress Cataloging-in-Publication Data
Paulsen, Gary.
Murphy's stand/Gary Paulsen and Brian Burks.
p. cm.
ISBN 0-8027-1277-0
I. Burks, Brian. II. Title.
PS3566.A834M88 1993
813'.54—dc20 93-1058
CIP

Printed in the United States of America

2 4 6 8 10 9 7 5 3 1

# MURPHY'S STAND

# CHAPTER 1

FATE IS AN odd thing; it cannot be controlled or altered; and fate gripped Al Murphy. Gripped him tighter than the death he had wished for—even longed for.

The big *grulla* horse plodded in the hot desert sun. Murphy had no idea of the part he was about to play, or the stand he was about to take, in what would eventually be known as the Turrett County War. Nor did he care.

Nothing mattered. Nothing.

The caring had stopped two—no—nearly three years ago. The day he buried his wife. He had never forgiven himself for her death. Midge was the only woman he had ever loved. After they married, he had resigned from his sheriff's job in Cincherville and she had left her café to go north in search of a new life, a peaceful life. They had found a secluded valley in Wyoming, built a cabin, and started a horse ranch. The ifs—always the ifs. If he had not gone into town for supplies and left her alone. . . . If he had taken her with him—if. . . .

Kneeling by her grave, he had placed the muzzle of the cocked Smith in his mouth. Only hate had kept him from pulling the trigger. Hate for the men that had caused her death and stolen their horses.

After he had methodically tracked and killed all seven of the men he was sure were responsible for Midge's death, he learned that a miner who had been shot by a young sheriff in Casper had Midge's rifle in his hands when he died. Was he the one who had chased her: who had caused her horse to stumble and fall, breaking her neck? Had the seven men been innocent? No, Murphy had told himself a

1

thousand times. They were guilty. They were vicious out-
laws who had deserved to die.

And so Murphy drifted, a slave to her memory. She was
dead, yet she lived. She lived in his mind, tormenting him
day and night with the caress of her fingertips, the feel of
her body, the scent of her auburn hair.

For the past few years he had been traveling around
with no purpose, no plans. Time and alcohol slowly
dimmed the pain, but life held no meaning.

The mouse-colored *grulla* raised his head and twitched
his left ear, which brought Murphy to think of the horse,
of the first time he had seen him and of the three aces and
two jacks he had drawn in the all-night poker game to win
him. But that was hundreds of miles ago, and the horse
was now only a skeleton of what he had been.

His hair showed no life, no luster. I ought to take better
care of him, Murphy thought. We should stop, stop somewhere, just for a while. Let the horse rest, let him gain
back some flesh. No other horse could have carried me
this far—on so little.

Murphy almost didn't see a faded road sign that was
partially hidden in a mesquite.

TURRETT—18 MILES

Turrett. A sorry name for a town, he thought. He
wondered if he had crossed the Arizona line. Or was he in
New Mexico Territory?

He gazed at the mountains before him to the east.
Eighteen miles. Four or five hours. That ought to put
Turrett high up in those mountains, or just on the other
side. He gave the *grulla* his head and gently spurred him.

Shortly the climb began. At first it was gradual, and the
countryside changed slowly. Greasewood and mesquite
gave way to dried yellow prairie grass with a smattering of
small crooked cedar trees, dwarfed by years of drought.

Occasionally a yucca thrust forth a green bundle of spears from the gray earth.

The road entered a narrow boulder-strewn canyon for the first abrupt ascent, using the ancient gravel streambed for passage. Murphy stopped and dismounted. He had been in the saddle since daylight and it was now midafternoon. His hip ached. The ache was always there, but worse when riding. It served as a constant reminder of the day he had killed the seven men and received the bullet wound.

He stretched his legs and looked at the cloudless sky. July, he thought, it must be close to the middle of July. The rains should have already started.

He reached for his canteen, took one long drink, and cupped his left hand to hold water for the *grulla*. It wasn't enough, but Murphy felt better.

He led the horse up the mountain, thinking there must be another way into Turrett, wherever Turrett was. The town had to have supplies, but the route before him was rough and seldom used.

Less than an hour later his legs were weak with the effort of walking up the incline.

A gunshot broke the silence.

Murphy froze.

Then another and another. The shots seemed close and echoed through the surrounding hills and canyons.

Murphy remained still, listening. Too many gunshots rang in his mind. Shots from yesterday. From his days as sheriff. And they usually spelled death.

His chest tightened and nervous energy filled the blood in his veins. He took the Smith from its holster and checked the loads, carefully pushing each primer in as he rotated the cylinder. Probably just somebody shooting at a deer, he thought, putting the heavy gun back in the holster. That's all.

He remained motionless a few minutes, listening, before he turned and mounted. There were no further shots.

The road climbed higher and the air began to change. It was crisper, fresher than below. Gradually the cedar trees disappeared and piñon and juniper now spotted the steep sides of the draw. The *grulla* began to breathe heavily and Murphy noticed sweat dripping from the horse's front shoulders.

Then he heard it.

Something from farther up the canyon. Over the horse's loud gasps came the noise again. Someone was coming. He listened and the sound grew louder. Several someones. And they were coming toward him fast.

The clatter of shod hooves on rocks grew louder. Murphy scanned his position. There was no place to run, no place to hide. Even if he wanted to.

Again his breath shortened and his muscles tightened reflexively. Then he saw them. Five of them.

The *grulla* raised his head and whinnied. Murphy tightened the reins and held him in the middle of the road.

The riders saw Murphy and pulled their horses into a trot. In a moment three men faced him. Two rode past and positioned themselves behind. They were rough men, Murphy knew. Long-riders—looking for trouble.

No one spoke immediately. Murphy stared into the eyes of a mustached man directly across from him, but he missed nothing. The color of the horses. The brand on the left shoulder—the men's faces.

These weren't cowboys. They were heavily armed, each with two revolvers, double cartridge belts, and a rifle in every scabbard. He felt the men behind him, felt their eyes glued to the center of his back.

"Who are you?" the mustached man asked. Murphy did not respond, nor did he shift his eyes. He kept his hands resting on the saddle horn, one over the other.

"Are you deaf—stupid?"

Murphy smiled.

A voice came from behind. "The man's talking to you."

The smile did not leave Murphy's lips. The mustached man became uneasy under Murphy's gaze. He was afraid, and Murphy sensed it.

But why should they fear him? Murphy had no chance against them. Not like this.

The shots, the earlier gunshots. Was that it? The fear was because of what he might know—or might find out.

Murphy slowly moved his right hand from the horn. It was time. These men were not going to let him go.

There was the swoosh of a rope in the air from behind. It startled the *grulla* and he jumped forward, hitting the mustached man's horse so hard it knocked the smaller sorrel to his knees. The end of the lariat loop dragged across the back of Murphy's neck and fell harmlessly behind.

Murphy lost one rein. Instinct took over. Survival. He set his spurs hard into the horse's belly. The trailing rein quickly snapped under the *grulla*'s running hooves. He pulled the Smith, turned in the saddle, and fired. A bullet stung his left ear. He fired until the gun clicked empty.

He heard shots behind him and he hugged the horse's neck, spurring. The *grulla* ran uphill with strength Murphy did not think he had—strength that threatened to burst the heart of the big horse.

They'll be coming, Murphy thought. They won't let me get away. They can't let me get away. Fierce rage enveloped him at the thought. Let 'em come. He pulled his rifle from the scabbard and rolled from the running horse.

The impact of the ground took the wind from him. He landed on his left shoulder, the rifle held tightly in his right hand above his head. His body slid across the gravel roadbed, which scratched and tore at his flesh.

He searched for a rock, a tree, anything close to get behind. There was nothing.

The riders were now in view. In seconds they would be upon him. Dirt exploded inches from his head, and the report of a gun reached him. In one motion he levered the .45–70 and rolled to his elbows. Bullets so close, too close, whined past.

There were no thoughts in his mind. Every movement was instinctive—the positioning of the rifle, the front bead visible in the rear sight and a man's chest both coming quickly into alignment.

He pulled the trigger and the heavy rifle kicked against his shoulder. The rider was lifted from the saddle by the impact of the bullet and seemed to hang in midair.

A bullet struck Murphy. There was no pain, just a heavy tug at his side. The .45–70 recoiled again. Another rider went down. They were too close now. There was no time to aim.

He rose to his feet and fired the remaining loads as fast as he could lever and pull the trigger. Bullets struck the ground and screamed through the air. The .45–70 clicked empty. It was over. He would die.

In that fraction of a second fate showed her hand. In unison, the three remaining riders wheeled their horses and fled. They don't know, thought Murphy. They had me—and they don't know.

He smiled and loaded the Smith, watching until only a hazy trail of dust remained from the disappearing horses.

Murphy held the Smith ready and walked toward the two men lying in the dirt. Both were dead. They lay facedown with holes in their backs as big as a man's fist.

Curious, he started to turn one man over, then stopped. A sickening feeling came over him. A hollowness in the guts. He wanted to leave, to ride on. He searched the area for the men's horses. They were not to be seen.

He started away, then turned back, and knelt beside one of the men. Money. They may have money. He grabbed the man's shoulder, then quickly released it. No. No. Whatever I am, whatever I've become, I'm no thief. Not even from dead men.

Murphy rose and wiped the side of his left cheek with his sleeve. Blood. He felt his ear and found where a bullet had grazed the upper rim.

It wasn't until he picked up his rifle and walked several hundred yards up the canyon that the muscles and nerves in his body began to return to normal and a dull ache came from his side. He stopped. Blood covered the side of his shirt. He set the rifle down and unbuttoned it. A bullet had cut a furrow a half inch deep in the flesh just above his hipbone.

"Not much to that," he said to himself. "Not much at all."

Over an hour later, Murphy topped a small rise, the *grulla*'s tracks becoming dim in the setting sunlight. A small meadow appeared in front of him, surrounded by the huge firs and pines characteristic of the high country. There was his horse, grazing contentedly on the lush green grass.

It was a pretty sight. A peaceful sight and Murphy thought of how the horse had saved him from the rope— from being dragged to death.

I don't mind dying, he thought. But not like that, not like a dog. He walked through the meadow toward the horse. A dark shape on the ground appeared in the corner of his eye. A shape that didn't fit, didn't belong.

He moved to it. A man lay face up in the tall grass. Murphy nudged him with his boot, then kneeled beside him. This was no ordinary man. He wore a black wool suit that looked new. His face was clean-shaven and his hair neatly trimmed—a handsome man. About my age, Murphy thought.

Two dark spots, one in the center of the belly and one above the heart showed the entrance of two bullets. Murphy opened the man's coat. No gun.

This is it, then, Murphy thought. This is what the shots were about—and why they had to kill me, or try.

Weariness gripped him. Exhaustion. Too much, too long, on too little. He rose to catch the *grulla*, started to mount, then stopped.

Over there is a very important man, he thought. Probably has family, a wife, children.

He scratched his chin. Can't be too far to Turrett. I should take him in before the coyotes and buzzards get at him. If someone doesn't find him soon, there won't be enough left to bury.

# CHAPTER 2

MURPHY HAD HIS arms around the upper portion of the
dead man's body, trying to drag him, to lift him up on the
*grulla*, when he heard horses coming from the east, from
the direction of Turrett.

He laid the man down. It can't be the long-riders, he
thought. They went west. Then who? Whoever it is—
they're in a hurry. They'll be here soon.

The thought hit him: They'll blame me for this. They'll
take me.

His body tightened. The weariness left and a numbing
energy began to flow through his veins. He scanned the
meadow, surprised at how quickly the dusk light had gone.

It was dark. Almost full dark.

Run, his brain told him. Run. But he could not. Would
not.

Moments later the riders arrived, almost passing him
while he stood quietly watching them in the still night air.

"Hey, over here," one of them yelled, seeing the *grulla*.

Murphy took a sack of Durham from his pocket and
shook some tobacco into a cigarette paper. He was gently
rolling the smoke between his fingers when four mounted
men stopped their horses beside him.

"Who are you?" one of the men asked.

Murphy carefully moved the edge of the cigarette paper
along the tip of his tongue.

"Who are you?" the man asked again.

"Look," Murphy said calmly. "I've already been through
this once today. Two men are dead. It's none of your
business."

9

The coolness—the sureness in Murphy's voice caused the man to hesitate. "I'm Dick Laker, sheriff of Turrett County. We're looking for a man. His horse came into town without him. Have you seen anyone?"

Murphy was surprised they hadn't noticed the body lying in front of him. Too dark, he guessed.

He lit a match with his thumbnail and moved it in cupped hands to his cigarette. At length, he answered, "The man. Would he be wearing fine clothes? A suit?"

"That's him," another voice spoke. "You've seen him then?"

With the cigarette hanging from his lips, Murphy drew the Smith. "I'll kill you, if you move. The man you're looking for. He's lying right in front of you."

No one moved—even breathed.

"I didn't kill him," Murphy continued. "I found him right where he is."

There was no doubt left in the sheriff's mind. Murphy was too calm—too controlled. He believed him. What's more, he believed that to move, to draw, was to die.

"I . . . I believe you," the sheriff said in a shaky voice. "Now, who are you?"

"Name's Murphy. Al Murphy. You can get down and take the body, but I'll have this gun on you. Any foolishness and I'll use it."

The men dismounted and in minutes they had the body tied onto a horse.

"You mentioned two other men," the sheriff said. "Two dead men?"

Murphy paused, thinking of the days when he was sheriff of Cincherville. He needs to know. I guess I better tell him.

He began. "I was headed toward Turrett from the west when I heard gunshots. Less than an hour later, five men, running their horses to the west, met and surrounded me. They had it in mind to kill me, there was no question.

"When it was over, two of them were dead. It was nearly dark when I reached this opening and found the dead man tied on your horse. I was taking him into town when you rode up."

Dick Laker was not new at being sheriff. For twenty years, twenty-three years to be exact, he had worn the badge of a lawman. He knew the words were truth—as sure as he knew that the man holding the gun was dangerous. Very dangerous. And for some reason—strange as it was in the night blackness—he trusted him.

"Murphy, put the gun away. I give my word that we won't move against you. I believe you."

"Your word." It was almost a whisper from Murphy's lips.

"Suit yourself," the sheriff answered. "But you're makin' a mistake. Turrett's the only town within eighty miles in any direction. You ought to ride in with us.

"Besides there'll be several people mighty interested in your story. Jake McCormick was a very influential man."

Eighty miles, Murphy thought. I haven't eaten for two, almost three days. The *grulla* would never make it. Not eighty miles. He holstered his gun. "I'll ride along. But if you change your mind about me, try to take me, I'll kill you."

A light, shivering sensation traveled the length of Dick Laker's spine. It had been years since he had heard a voice so cold, so sure and deadly. Again, he knew the words were true.

Murphy rode behind as the horses traveled at a walk. What have I gotten myself into, he thought. Where will this road take me? I wish I could leave, just travel on. None of this is my business.

Soon the horses topped out and in the distance below he saw lights he knew must be the town of Turrett. Food. Grain. A drink and a bath. His right hand touched his empty pocket, reminding him he was broke—penniless.

The town was large and prosperous looking compared to most he had been in. A lighted sign from a large two-story building to his right caught his eye.

MCCORMICK MERCANTILE

Not anymore, he thought. The town was quiet. Even the two saloons showed no signs of overly rambunctious activity. Must not be a cow or mining town, Murphy thought. They stopped in front of a small brick building with weathered, dull letters spelling the word "Sheriff" on the door.

Dick Laker spoke to his men. "Slim, better take McCormick to the undertaker. Troy, get Jake's sister, Christine. Don't tell her anything, just bring her here. Jay, put the horses up. Be sure and give Murphy's horse double grain."

Murphy stepped from his horse, retrieved his rifle and saddlebags, and followed the sheriff into the jail. Inside, Laker moved to his desk and sat down. He watched Murphy, appraising him.

Murphy was tall—well over six feet. His worn and dirty clothes fit loosely on his body, telling of a time when he weighed more, a lot more. His sideburns and beard were heavily smattered with gray, making him look much older than he was.

The eyes, that's what made Murphy different from any man the sheriff had ever seen. They were light blue. Strange eyes that seemed to see through whatever they were fixed upon.

"Looks like those two men you mentioned weren't the only ones that got shot," Laker said, noticing the dried blood in Murphy's beard and a large bloodstain on the side of his shirt.

The sheriff opened his desk drawer and took out a quart of whiskey. "You take a pull on that. A long pull. Looks like you need it."

He pointed to a corner of the room. "There's a washbasin over there, a pitcher of water, and some soap. Help yourself."

While Murphy washed, he felt a warm comfort start to grow in his empty belly. He liked the feeling. That was the problem, he had liked it too much—so much that he had spent the last couple of years seldom drawing a sober breath.

Until six months ago, when his stomach finally gave out and the bleeding made him stop. Since then, he drank, but not like before.

Whiskey doesn't take long when you're running on empty, he thought. And I been empty way too long.

Murphy hardly recognized himself in the small broken mirror above the washbasin. He asked himself how long it had been since he'd shaved or had a haircut. Three months? No, maybe four or five or a hundred. Who cared? What difference did it make?

He'd finished combing his long brown hair when a man came into the office with a woman. An exceptionally pretty woman.

"Here she is," the deputy said.

"Thanks, Troy." The man turned to leave when Laker stopped him. "Troy, looks like I'm gonna be tied up awhile. Find Slim and make the rounds with him."

"Christine, I'd like you to meet Al Murphy," Laker gestured toward the corner.

Murphy stepped toward her. She wore a full-length blue cotton dress, buttoned to her neck. The dress could not hide her lovely full figure. Large green eyes met his and for a moment neither spoke. Her gaze was friendly, but direct. Murphy nodded his head. "Nice to meet you."

Laker moved a chair. "Christine, please sit down."

"It's about Jake, isn't it, Sheriff? Something's happened. I know it. I sat on the porch after supper with Sarah, waiting for Jake to come home. I knew something was wrong then."

"Christine," Laker began, "Jake's horse came into town without him an hour or so before dark. I talked to your store clerk. He said Jake was complaining about being cooped up in the store all the time, said he couldn't get no air. Said he was going to ride the Twin Lake country, look for some of his cattle, and would go on home from there."

Laker shifted his weight and his chair squeaked. "I got a few men and we rode west—staying on the old road. It was almost plumb dark when we rode up on this man," he pointed at Murphy. "You want to tell the story from here?"

"No, Sheriff. You're doing fine."

"What has happened?" Christine said, rising. "Jake's dead, isn't he?"

Tears fell from her eyes. Laker stepped to her and put his arm around her.

Murphy took the bottle from the desk and retreated to the corner. It bothered him. Bothered him more than he cared to admit—even to himself.

"I'm sorry, Christine," Laker said in a low voice. "I really am. I liked Jake. You know that. We all liked him."

At last she regained her composure and sat back down. Laker took a cup from his desk, went to Murphy, and filled it with whiskey. He drank the cupful in one pull, then filled it again and walked back to Christine. "Drink some of this."

"No," she said, her voice trembling. "No. I'll be fine. Tell me what happened. I have to know."

The sheriff paused, then recounted the story Murphy had told him.

When he finished she spoke. "It was Bernard Gibson's hired killers, Sheriff. You know that. No one else would do this. Jake had no other enemies. I want Gibson arrested for murder. I want him arrested now."

"Now, Christine," Laker said. "You know I can't do that,

not without proof. Tomorrow we're ridin' to get the two men Murphy said he killed. Maybe we'll find something. Maybe we can backtrack 'em. You know I'll do everything I can."

She glared at him. "Sheriff, you haven't done anything in years."

"I saw a Rocking G brand on the left shoulder of a couple of the horses," Murphy interrupted from the corner. "Don't know if that helps you any."

Christine looked Laker straight in the eyes. "You know that's Gibson's brand. How much proof do you need? You know the trouble Jake and I have had ever since we opened the mercantile in competition with him. Over a fourth of our cattle have been shot or stolen. Two freight wagons were held up, one driver killed. Who'll be next?"

She took a breath. "There are over twenty men at the ranch. They're not going to take this lightly. Jake and I were good to them and they know it."

She pointed a finger at Laker. "Bernard Gibson and his hired guns have already been allowed to ride roughshod over this town way too long. You had better do something, something quick, Sheriff. If you don't, those men will."

Murphy watched from the corner, the warm feeling now in his brain. Laker was obviously rattled by her words. He knew the implications of what she said. This thing could get big—real big—in a hurry.

"Now, Christine," Laker said. "Don't do anything foolish. I'll have to ask you to control your men. I'll do everything humanly possible to find the killers and bring them to justice. You know I will."

She stood. Her face was red and determination filled her puffy eyes. "Sheriff, do you want to go home with me and tell Jake's wife and children that he's dead? Would you like to stay there and listen to their cries throughout the night?"

Laker looked down at his feet.

"No. I didn't think so," she continued, "You haven't got much time, Sheriff. If I were you, I'd make the best of it."

Christine was almost to the door when she turned and looked into the dim corner where Murphy stood. "Mr. Murphy, I thank you for what you've done. I don't know who you are, or where you come from, but you're in this now. Gibson is not going to like some stranger coming into town and killing his men. They'll be after you. They won't rest until they've settled the score."

Murphy did not respond. Her gaze lingered a few moments longer before she grasped the doorknob. "Somehow, Mr. Murphy, I think they'll have their hands full—when they go after you."

The door closed behind her and the sheriff moved to his chair and sat down. His face was tense, anxious. Murphy understood Laker's predicament as few other men could, and he sympathized with the bald, heavyset man.

He had seen other lawmen who reminded him of Laker. Men who in their younger days were some of the best. But the passage of years had unnerved them. The older they were, the more afraid of death they became, and the less it really mattered.

Murphy began to think of things he would do if he were sheriff. Quickly he caught himself. He thought, Why should I care?

The initial effect of the whiskey had slowly changed and it now left Murphy exhausted. He picked up his gear and started for the door.

"Where are you going?" the sheriff asked.

"I'm worn out. Figured I'd find somewhere to rest awhile. Thanks for the drink."

Laker rose. "You hungry?"

Murphy hesitated before answering. "Yeah."

"We'll go to the Hash House. Best stew you ever ate." The sheriff reached for his hat.

"Well—ah—no," Murphy stuttered. "Guess I'll pass and just hole up somewhere."

Laker didn't have to ask the question, he knew the answer. "I'm buying," he said cheerfully. "And afterward you can bunk right here. Besides, I want you close so you can ride with us in the mornin'."

The sheriff started to open the door. Murphy caught his arm. "No. I won't be going with you tomorrow. This is your business, not mine. I'll be leaving as soon as my horse has rested awhile."

"Didn't you hear Christine?" Laker said. "You're in this. Like it or not."

"I heard, but she's wrong. I'm not—in—anything. I did what I had to do. That's all. Like I said, I'll be leaving."

# CHAPTER 3

BRIGHT SUNLIGHT FLOODED through the cell window on Al Murphy's face, waking him. The bunk felt good and he was not anxious to leave it. Sun's too bright, he thought. What time is it?

He lay there several minutes before turning to get up. A sharp pain came from his side. He gritted his teeth and groaned as he sat upright and pulled his shirt open. The area around the bullet wound in his side was swollen and purple. "Guess it's worse than I thought," he murmured to himself.

Pulling his boots on, he went into the office and looked at the clock on the wall. Two in the afternoon. Can't be. I couldn't have slept that long. He looked out the window. The shadows showed the sun to be high.

After washing his face, he took his shirt and tried to wash the wound. He had no more than started when the office door opened and Christine walked through. He hastily reached for his shirt and put it on. "Sorry, I should have knocked," she said.

"That's all right. I'm gettin' too late a start on the day."

"Has the sheriff been back?" she asked.

"No, at least I haven't seen him."

She moved over to the desk and sat on the edge.

Murphy watched her while he buttoned his shirt. She looked different from last night. She wore a brown riding skirt, brown corduroy work shirt, and high-heeled black boots. He liked the difference. Her eyes turned to his.

"Mr. Murphy. Jake and I were partners in the mercantile. Now that he's gone, I have to take care of things he normally would have handled." She hesitated a moment. "Would you like a job?"

The question shook him for a moment and his mind raced through her conversation with the sheriff last night. His first response was to say no. Then he cataloged his situation. Broke. One poor horse. Nowhere to go and nobody expecting him anywhere in this world. Still, he hesitated.

Her gaze was direct—unshifting. Finally, he spoke. "I might."

"I need a man to ride shotgun with my freight. Two drivers quit this morning, after learning about Jake's death. I convinced one of them to stay by promising him someone would go with him. Good mule skinners are hard to find. I could take a man or two from the ranch, but I am about to be shorthanded there too."

She moved her eyes to the floor. "Most of the men are loyal—and angry. But three of my ranch hands also quit this morning. I can't blame them. They hadn't worked for us long, and they knew that trouble was becoming more likely with each day."

Murphy moved a few steps to face her. "I heard about one of your freight drivers last night."

Her eyes lifted and her glare was cold. "Are you afraid?"

Pride, the silly pride men are born with, clouded his judgment. And stupidity. The kind that only a truly beautiful woman can bring about in a man.

"I'll take the job. But I'm no hand with mules." He couldn't believe his words.

"Good. You won't have to be." Her lips relaxed. "Fort Crosston is eighty-three miles east of here. Your work will be to see that the goods are delivered to the fort. One load a week."

"Government contract?" he queried.

"Yes, that's part of the trouble. Gibson Mercantile had the contract since the fort was built, about four years ago.

They also had the beef contract for the Apache Indian Reservation. Gibson's flour, meal, and goods were of poor quality, but the post had no choice but to deal with him— until Jake bid and won the contract."

"You provide the beef too?"

"Yes, if there's any left by this fall. Gibson's murdering cowards have hit us once a week for over a month. It's taking a toll."

She moved from the desk. "A wagon will be loaded and ready for you at dawn tomorrow. Pay is twenty dollars a week. You can have the first week's salary in advance. Just tell the clerk at the store that I sent you."

He stopped her on the porch. "You won't make any money. You can't pay me that much, pay a driver too, and come out."

"No, but we will hold the contract and break even. That's all we can hope for—at least for now."

Murphy watched her turn and walk away. She had a proud look, a certain arrogance about her, but he liked it. When she left the shade of the boardwalk, her long blond hair shone in the sunlight.

As he strapped on his gun belt, inside the jail, he thought how foolish he had been to take the job. But I am broke—and hungry. And so's my horse.

After checking on the *grulla*, Murphy approached the McCormick Mercantile, conscious of his empty belly. The building was impressive. Great pains had been taken to build the large wooden structure. The clerk was a small man with round wire-rim glasses resting loosely on his thin, pointed nose.

"How can I help you?"

Murphy didn't answer. Instead he searched the room. Everything that could possibly be needed on a farm or ranch was there. He liked the mingled smells of the new leather and the sorghum grain.

"I'm Al Murphy. Jake's sister, Christine, hired me to

ride on the Fort Crosston run. She said I could have a week's advance."

"Certainly, Mr. Murphy."

"Is—is Christine married?" Al asked.

The clerk smiled. "No. But lots of young men are trying to change that. None of them seem to measure up to her standards. At least not yet."

"What are her standards?"

The store clerk winked. "I don't know. I doubt if even she knows. It'll be a lucky man that gets that woman."

Almost four hours later, Murphy stood in his room and stared in the mirror at a man who looked older than his thirty-two years.

He had eaten, bought a new set of clothes—except boots—found a bathhouse and bathed, been to a doctor who packed and bandaged his side, paid for a week's feed and care for the *grulla*, bought a bottle of cheap whiskey, which lay on the bed, and rented this room in the Horrell Hotel for the night. Four dollars and seventy three cents still remained in his right pants pocket.

"I guess it's time," he said out loud, fingering his gray-streaked black beard. He stopped by the bed and took a long pull on the bottle before going downstairs. In the street, he was surprised at the soft dusk light. Must be six or better in the evening, he thought. May not be a barber open.

He found the only shop in town. A thick-necked, red-headed man stood outside locking the door when Murphy stepped up.

"Sorry, I'm closed," the man said without looking around.

"Well, I knew I was late. I'll give you two bits extra if you'll open back up and give me a shave and haircut."

The barber hesitated, then turned and opened the door. Forty minutes later, Murphy stepped out into the darkness. A breeze blew across his face. It felt cool. It had been a long time since he had felt this good.

He counted the remainder of his money. Plenty for supper, he thought, and a little left over too. I believe I'll have me a steak, the biggest steak in town. Kind of celebrate.

Murphy was not far from the Hash House when the sheriff and three men rode by in the street. Two horses trailed, loaded with tarped bundles that Murphy knew were the men he had killed.

Somehow, that seemed so long ago, so distant, yet he knew it was only yesterday. He waved to Laker. The sheriff turned his head toward him, but offered no acknowledgment. After they had passed, Murphy stroked his clean-shaven face. I guess he didn't recognize me. Then another thought came to him: Gibson and his men might not recognize me either. He grinned.

After supper, he stood outside the diner, enjoying the smoke he had rolled. There's nothing—well, almost nothing—any better than a good smoke after a fine meal, he thought. All too soon the cigarette burned short and he couldn't hold it any longer. He flicked it into the street.

Curiosity tugged at him. How had the sheriff made out? Why had it taken him so long? Did they find out anything new? What were Laker's plans? He walked down the boardwalk toward the jail. Part of his brain told him to go to his room, to leave it alone and mind his own business.

The curiosity won, mostly because he felt too good, too alive to go to bed now in an empty room. Besides, there wasn't anything else to do but get drunk in a saloon or find a card game, neither of which he wanted to do.

Laker had his head on his desk between his hands when Murphy quietly opened the door. At the squeak of a hinge, the sheriff raised his head.

"How'd it go?" Murphy asked.

"What do you mean, how'd it go? Who in tarnation are you?"

"Murphy, Al Murphy."

Laker sat back in the chair. "You sure have changed in a hurry. You don't look anything like the saddle tramp that stayed here last night."

"Well, I got cleaned up a little. So, how'd you come out?"

"No good. Oh, we found the men you killed, all right. The buzzards had already started on 'em. But they didn't have anything, no papers—nothing that tied them to Gibson. We backtracked to where they killed McCormick. Like you said, there was five of 'em. Found two .44 bullet casings."

Laker shifted his weight and the chair creaked. "Their tracks was clear for three miles, going straight for Gibson's ranch in the Malpies. Thought we had him until the tracks disappeared.

"Cattle covered them. A whole herd went through. We spent the rest of the day trying to find where the five horses came out. We never did."

Murphy wanted to ask why he hadn't split up the men and had someone follow the three riders' tracks west, but he controlled his tongue. "Looks like you're the one that could use a drink tonight."

"I could—sure could. You drank all I had."

"Come on, I'll buy."

"Where did you get so almighty rich all of a sudden?" Laker asked.

"I got a job."

"Yeah, and doing what?"

"Riding along with a freight wagon. Pays good. A real pretty boss, too."

The sheriff smiled. "Looks like you've already spent a month's wages. Probably just as well. If you're ridin' Mc-

Cormick wagons, you may not live to see another payday. I'm glad you're enjoying it."

Later that night as Murphy lay in bed a picture came to his mind before he drifted to sleep. Beautiful green eyes and long blond hair. And for the first night in a long time, Midge was gone.

# CHAPTER 4

CHRISTINE STOOD BY the loaded wagon in the faint dawn light. Murphy approached her. "You're up and around awful early," he said with a smile.

She stared at him.

"Something wrong?" he asked. "You don't look too happy."

The voice, if it had not been for his voice, she would not have had a clue who he was. "I'm sorry, you've changed. I didn't recognize you."

"Is it a good change or a bad one?"

"It's—it's good." She looked him up and down. Her eyes sparkled and she smiled. "Except for your hat. You are going to have to do something about it."

"Well," he drawled. "If this outfit would pay a man a little more, he could afford a new hat. What are you doing here this early anyway?"

"I had to see—see if you would take the money and leave, or be here like we agreed."

"You sure do have faith in a man's word, don't you? And I appreciate it. I really do. Most women, they aren't trusting. But you—well, it's reassuring to know that you're diffcrent."

Her smile left. She walked around the wagon. A small, wiry-looking man came out from an alley beside the store, leading two mules. She met him and took the mules' lead ropes. "Skeet, I'd like for you to meet Mr. Murphy. He will be going with you this trip."

The old man spit a stream of thick tobacco juice to the side before speaking. "Can you shoot?"

"If I have to," Murphy replied.

"That ain't what I asked." Skeet cocked his hat to the side and scratched his head. "I ain't goin' if you can't shoot. Can you hit anything? Yes or no, that's all I want to know. Yes or no."

"Depends," Murphy said, grinning.

"Now you listen to me, young feller—"

"Skeet," Christine interrupted. "You had better go get the other mules."

The old man muttered as he left. "I don't see why no one can answer a simple question around here. Yes or no. That's all I wanted to know."

"Don't pay any attention to him," Christine told Murphy. "He's a good man, one of the best mule skinners I've ever seen. He grumbles a lot, but he doesn't mean anything by it."

Murphy watched Christine and Skeet collar, position, and hook the traces to the eight mules, surprised at her ability. Not a movement was wasted and she was every bit as fast as the old man.

Soon the work was done. Skeet walked past and went into the store. He returned with a double-barreled Greener ten-gauge shotgun and a box of shells. He climbed onto the wagon seat and looked down at Murphy.

"I wouldn't have to take this," he said, patting the gun, "if you could talk. Yes or no. That's all I want to know."

Murphy grinned and stood to the side. "Does the company provide bullets? I could use a box of .44s and one of .45–70s."

Christine went into the store and returned with the shells. She handed them to Murphy and for a moment their eyes met.

"You coming?" Skeet asked. "We ain't got forever you know."

"Yeah, I'm coming." Murphy smiled at Christine, then turned and climbed onto the wagon. He was barely seated before Skeet popped the long, heavy reins. A ripple traveled to the lead mules and in an instant they started to pull.

"Get along, jack. Get along now," Skeet hollered.

"You kinda like that one, don't you, young feller?" Skeet said. "I like her too . . . only different. But that's only because I'm old. If I was younger, I'd sure enough give her a chase. I'd . . ."

Murphy wasn't listening. His thoughts were fixed and deep on the woman behind. The sun peeped above the eastern horizon and spread its warm rays on them. The terrain on this side of the mountain was much gentler than the abrupt sides of the western face, and the going was much easier.

The mules were fresh and wanted to trot, but Skeet held them back. The road was well traveled. It followed a wide ridge and went downhill gradually. Grama grass covered the earth, spotted by an occasional cedar, yucca, or cactus.

"What kind of gun you got?" Skeet asked.

"A Winchester .45-70."

"Well, is it any good? Can you hit anything?"

Here we go again, thought Murphy. Two jackrabbits suddenly ran across the road, one a little in front of the other. Without hesitation Murphy grabbed the Winchester, stood, levered, and fired.

Two shots, fired so quickly they almost sounded as one. The gunfire startled the mules and they took off at a run. Murphy was knocked back on to the seat.

"Whoa, whoa, mules," Skeet yelled and pulled the reins with all his might. At length the mules responded, set back into a trot, and stopped.

Skeet was excited. He set the wagon brake and stood. "What in tarnation is wrong with you? Look what you done. Are you dimwitted? Plumb thick between the ears? It's a wonder I stopped 'em as quick as I did. What kind of a fool stunt was that? Are you trying to get us both killed?"

"You're the one that keeps on asking if I can hit any-thing. I thought maybe if I showed you, you'd shut up."

"What'd you shoot at?"

"Two rabbits."

"I didn't see 'em. Did you hit 'em?"

"Yeah."

"I don't believe you did. I didn't see no rabbits." Skeet climbed to the ground. "You come show me. I don't think you shot nothin'."

"I don't care what you think, old man," Murphy said. "They're there, two or three hundred yards back, on the left. Go look for yourself."

"I will, and them rabbits better be there."

Skeet left, grumbling. "Young fool. Rabbits—I don't believe it. I never seen no rabbits and . . ."

Murphy removed a Durham sack from his pocket and rolled a cigarette. The sun was warm through his clothes. Going to be hot today, he thought. After a few deep draws on the smoke, he let it hang from his lips and replaced the two spent cartridges in his rifle.

He heard Skeet talking to himself, and shortly the little man climbed onto the seat beside him. "Yes or no. That's all you had to say. No use in scarin' the mules that way."

Skeet released the brake and popped the reins. To Murphy's surprise, he quit talking. Over a mile later, the old man spit and smiled. "Was pretty good shootin', though. Not enough of them rabbits left to make soup. Hair still floatin' in the air."

Presently they met a wagon drawn by two horses. A man, woman, and two children waved and passed by them without stopping.

At noon, Skeet turned the mules off the road and followed two narrow ruts that led to a large cottonwood tree. "We'll take dinner here and rest the mules awhile," he said.

They ate canned peaches in the shade of the tree. A

slight breeze picked up. "Liable to rain this evenin'," Skeet said. "I feel it. It's in the air."

Something shone briefly on a low, treeless hill in the distance, catching Murphy's attention. Seconds later it was gone. Probably a rock, he thought. But a rock wouldn't shine . . .

Murphy thought of the things he knew about the trouble between McCormick and Gibson. Christine's warning from the night before came to him: "Gibson won't take the killing of his men lightly." Besides that, McCormick freight wagons seemed to have become a regular target lately, and they had double reason to hit this one.

The thought came: They will hit us. It's almost a certainty if they know I'm here. Do they know? Could the change in my appearance have fooled them?

No. If Gibson is serious about running the mercantile out of business he has spies everywhere. He knows. He'd make it his business to know.

"Skeet," Murphy said. "How many miles will we travel today?"

"About twenty-five, twenty-six. This part of the goin' is about the easiest."

"Where will we camp tonight?"

"Same place I always do. There's a seep spring in a narrow draw. Enough water and feed for the mules, and the sides kind of holds 'em in close."

Murphy was quiet a few minutes before he spoke again. "Is there water anywhere else?"

"Nope, that's it—unless it rains, which it's goin' to. What's all the questionin' about? You figurin' on trouble?"

"No, not really," Murphy lied. "Just wanted to know how things were laid out."

There was no reason to excite Skeet. It would serve no purpose now. He would tell him later, if and when it became necessary

Soon they left. The road maintained an easterly direction and dropped in elevation with each mile until they reached the flat of the desert. Greasewood, mesquite, and cactus now dominated the land, looking much the same to Murphy as the desert he had crossed on the west side of the mountain a few days earlier.

Murphy constantly scanned the countryside for anything peculiar. He looked at the sun. An hour, maybe an hour and a half before sundown, he thought. The seep can't be too far ahead. We'll hitch the mules back up after they've watered and travel four or five miles farther before we stop for the night. It won't stop an ambush, but it should frustrate their effort.

Clouds, mixed with an occasional streak of lightning, gathered on the eastern horizon. The team took the wagon down into the head of a draw and Murphy saw several salt cedars below and to the right. That must be the seep, he thought.

A stiff wind started to blow. Skeet stopped the team on the only level place available and set the wagon brake. He climbed down and looked up at Murphy. "Well, you goin' to help, or just sit there? Young folks—won't work, won't help, won't do nothin'."

Murphy did not like it, the feeling in his gut. Too many times the tightness, a hollow queasiness inside, had warned him of impending danger. But what could he do? It might rain, and it might not. Right now, the clouds were miles away and the mules had to have water. Once on the ground, the feeling grew stronger. He took his rifle from the seat.

"Skeet, you better load your Greener and stay with the mules. I want to look around some before we water."

"A-course I'll load my gun. Do you think I'm a dad-burn idiot? Checkin' the water is the first smart thing you've done since I knowed you."

The night was fast approaching. Murphy stayed high and walked the ridge of the draw. The salt cedars below

MURPHY'S STAND ■ 31

swayed and shook vigorously in the ever-increasing wind. He could not see the water.

He levered a load into his rifle and left the hammer cocked. His eyes briefly left the draw to search the horizon. There was a movement in the distance: a horse and rider, running up a hill. In seconds they topped over and were out of sight.

A spy, Murphy thought. Making sure we're where they think we should be. Are there any more? Somebody could easily be hidden in the salt cedars below. One way to find out. He lay flat on the ground and fired three quick shots into the cedars.

There was no answer to his shots. No activity. The tension in his body eased somewhat and he went into the draw before moving back up to the wagon.

"What's all the shootin'?" Skeet asked. "What'd you see?"

"Nothing much. I saw a—"

"What do you mean, nothin'? You just go down there and start shootin'. Don't see a thing, just start shootin' at who knows what."

Skeet took his hat off and threw it on the ground. "And here I am—hearin' the shots and gettin' ready to blast anybody that comes out of there. Nothin' . . ."

"Skeet," Murphy said sharply. "Listen. I saw a man on horseback. I think he might be a spy. We need to hurry and water the mules. Then I've got a plan . . ."

"Well, did you hit him?" Skeet asked as he unbuckled the harness.

"Hit who?"

"The spy, of course. Who else would you be shootin' at?"

"I didn't shoot at anyone."

"Nobody. You didn't shoot at nobody. Just shot at nothin'. Just . . ."

Murphy stopped listening. His mind turned to his plan. A thin smile spread slowly across his lips.

# CHAPTER 5

MURPHY AND SKEET quickly watered the mules, two at a time, and took them back to the wagon. Murphy had decided to stay and make camp at the spring, at least for a few hours. He had never been good at running or hiding, and he planned a welcome for the guests he felt were sure to come.

"Skeet. Can you lead eight mules by yourself?"

"Of course I can't. Nobody can. I'd have to tail 'em. Then I could."

"Okay, tail them."

"Why? What are you figurin' on?"

"We have to hurry. I'm certain Gibson's men will hit us tonight. They want to stop the freight, but more than that, they want me."

"Why? Why would they want you?"

"It's a long story," Murphy said. "I killed two of Gibson's men, but there's no time for all that now. I want you to tail the mules and lead them a half mile or better away. Keep the Greener with you. Shoot anyone you see and don't leave unless I call your name."

"What are you gonna do?"

"I'm going to build a fire in front of the wagon and make a couple of bedrolls. Then, I'm going to go to the top of the ridge, lie down, and wait. When they come, I'll be here to greet them."

With Murphy's help, Skeet quickly tied each mule's lead rope to the tail of the next, making four mules to the string. Two of the mules kicked, but Skeet stayed to the side and rammed his knee in their bellies. That stopped their nonsense.

Skeet carried his shotgun in his left hand and led the two mule strings in his right. Soon the night enveloped him and he was gone.

Murphy hurriedly gathered some dry mesquite and salt cedar limbs for a fire. The darkness made the task difficult. At length, a fire blazed in front of the wagon and two stuffed bedrolls could easily be seen, one to each side.

Murphy took his rifle and carefully climbed the low swell the wagon had descended. At the top, he went south about fifty yards to gain an even higher vantage point. He lay down under a large greasewood.

The setup looks good, he thought. All I have to do is wait. They'll come.

Lightning streaked the sky, followed by a faraway rumble; the wind smelled of rain. Skeet was right, the storm's coming. Murphy grinned. They'll make their move soon. As soon as the fire has died down some and they think we're asleep.

The howl of the wind annoyed him: he could not hear above it, would not know of their approach.

The fire burned low and tiny specks of rain began to travel with the wind. A bolt of lightning struck close, and in its brief light he thought he saw something move on the ridge opposite him. Thunder crackled through the sky, then a noise came from behind him. A sound that was not in place with that of the wind.

Footsteps?

Murphy held the loaded rifle tightly in his hands, but he found himself wanting the Smith. The steps—if that's what they were—stopped. He's too close, Murphy thought. I can't move, can't breath, let alone reach for my sidearm. I can't let him know I'm here.

A flash appeared across from him and the simultaneous

report of a gun rang out. In an instant a shot came from behind him, almost beside him.

A barrage of shots and muzzle flashes followed. They seemed to come from everywhere. Murphy braced himself, threw his body sideways and over, and fired the Winchester at the man behind him. Lightning flashed, and in that tiny fraction of a second he saw a look of bewilderment on the man's face. The man lingered a moment, teetering back and forth before he fell to the ground.

Murphy did not waste a second. He lay facedown, rested his left elbow on the ground, and steadied his rifle. Coolly, instinctively, he guessed at where the rifle sights were in the darkness and fired at each muzzle flash.

A man on the far ridge screamed. Out of the corner of his right eye Murphy saw a flash. He turned, leveled his rifle, and waited. Again the flash came, and instantly he sighted and squeezed the trigger. The .45-70 kicked against his shoulder.

Murphy knew the attackers were about to realize their mistake, that they were about to pinpoint his location. He had to move—move now.

He ran to the right, crashing through brush in the blackness. Gunfire bellowed around him. He threw himself on the ground and leveled the rifle. He saw a flash and squeezed the trigger. The hammer on the rifle clicked empty.

He laid the long gun down and grabbed the Smith with his right hand. With his left he fumbled in his shirt pocket for bullets.

Another flash and he fired. It was different now—the coolness, the sureness was gone. At close range he trusted the speed and accuracy of the revolver. But the fifty- and sixty-yard targets he now shot at left him wondering about the placement of his bullets—and Murphy did not like to wonder.

He holstered the Smith, grabbed the rifle, and rolled several yards to the left. One, two, three. Murphy counted the shells his fingers deftly pushed into the rifle magazine.

Then he felt it. Even before his brain registered the lack of gunshots, he felt the quiet, the stillness around him.

Heavy rain began to fall and he quit counting the shells but continued to fill the rifle. He pulled his hat low over his forehead to protect his face.

The rain became heavier, drenching him. Nothing could be seen in the blackness. No coals from the fire, no muzzle flashes, not even the rifle positioned across his lap.

It was over, Murphy knew. How many? How many could he have hit? It happened fast, like it always did. He tried to remember his shots, the imaginary sights he saw each time he had squeezed the trigger. Again he counted, this time men.

Three. At least three, maybe four, he said to himself. He rose from the ground. He felt no remorse. He had not gone to murder them while they slept. They had come and they had received the proper reward for their actions.

"Cowards," he said aloud.

Lightning hit close. A tingling sensation went through his body and a clasp of thunder deafened his ears. He quickly moved down the slope, stumbling and falling twice before he found the wagon and took refuge beneath it.

Murphy smiled, his thoughts on Skeet. He's out there somewhere, hidden with the mules. He'll be mad, but there's nothing I can do until the rain passes. I'd never find him and he can't hear my calls in this.

Murphy lay down in the water and mud, using his hat for a pillow. The adrenaline that pumped in his body slowly receded, leaving him tired. He was almost asleep when he heard the rain stop.

Stars shone, and it looked like the storm had never been. He crawled from under the wagon and walked in the direction Skeet had gone, calling his name every so often. It took a while, and he walked farther than the distance he thought Skeet would have gone. Then he heard him.

"I'm over here." The words were barely audible. "Over here."

Murphy almost ran into Skeet before he saw the shape of the mules behind him.

"Sounded like a war," Skeet said anxiously. "I was plumb sure you was dead. Nobody could've lived through that much shootin'."

Murphy grinned. "I'm afraid our bedrolls took a heck of a beating."

"Did you get 'em? Did you get some of 'em?"

"Yeah."

"How many was they? Did you see 'em come in? Was they Gibson's men? Bet they was surprised."

"Yeah, I think so."

"Well, are you gonna tell me what happened? Leave me out here in the rain all night long holdin' mules, and won't even tell me what all went on. If you was me, wouldn't you want to know—?"

"I will tell you," Murphy said, "but right now we better hitch the mules and travel on. We'll stop and rest awhile about daylight."

"I ain't ate or nothin'," Skeet grumbled as they walked. "Here I am, soakin' wet and hungry. Does he care? Naw. He don't care."

Soon the mules were hitched and the tattered, bullet-riddled bedrolls loaded. The beauty of the night, the magnificence of the star-filled sky wrapped around them. The mules plodded forward and Murphy felt an awe about it all. His life, any life, seemed so insignificant, so meaningless, compared to the splendor of the world around him.

Skeet was quiet now, except for an occasional spit to the side. The rhythm of the mules' hooves had a lethargic effect on Murphy. His head nodded and his chin bobbed up and down on his chest with each bump.

Hours later, a faint, almost invisible gray light appeared in front of them on the eastern horizon. Skeet stopped the mules and shook Murphy's shoulder. "Well, it's daylight, ain't it? You said we'd stop at daylight."

Murphy stared into the night and yawned. "Looks dark to me."

"Can't you see? Ain't you got eyes? The sun's comin' up."

"Okay," Murphy said quietly. "Go ahead and stop." Then he dozed off.

"No you don't, young feller. You get off this here wagon and help unhitch and hobble them mules. They need to rest and graze a spell, though they ain't much grass here. Besides, what about me? Don't I never get to rest or eat or anythin'?"

Murphy stepped sleepily from the wagon. Thirty minutes later the mules had been cared for and both men lay on top of their bedrolls, snoring.

# CHAPTER 6

IT WAS MIDAFTERNOON on the third day since they had left Turrett. Murphy and Skeet saw a long, green, snakelike valley a few miles ahead. "There she is," Skeet said. "The Little Creek and Fort Crosston."

The remainder of the trip had been uneventful, except for the screams of a nearby mountain lion and Skeet's blast from his ten-gauge into the brush. They had seen only one other traveler, a lone man riding west.

"Skeet, what can you tell me about Fort Crosston?"

"Nothin'. I can't tell you nothin'. Just like you don't tell me nothin'."

"I'll tell you anything you want to know. All you have to do is ask."

"I did ask. You never told me nothin' about all the shootin' the other night. You just left me out there in the rain."

Murphy told Skeet all he knew of the events two nights ago. "Okay. Now I've told you the story. What can you tell me about Fort Crosston?"

"It's a fort."

"I know it's a fort, Skeet. How'd it get its name? What's it doing out here?"

"Five, six years ago there was an Indian fight. A big one. A captain name Crosston was killed. They named the fort after him. That's why it's here. To make the Apaches behave themselves."

"Where's the reservation?"

"About sixteen miles south. Real purty place, too. In the mountains. Lots of water and game."

"Are there any settlers around? Ranches? Farms?"

"Gettin' to be. There's lots of water in the Little Creek, runnin' right by the fort. About twenty miles north is the Two Rivers country. All that country is bein' settled. They farm, and the fort pays good for their crops and stock."

Murphy gazed at the miragelike valley ahead. They did not seem to be getting any closer. Distances in the desert were hard to judge, especially through the waves of heat.

"Well?" Skeet said.

"Well what?"

"Ain't you gonna ask me no more questions? You ain't gonna talk to me no more?"

"How far's the fort from here?"

"Ain't far. Two, three miles. Less than an hour."

"That's all I want to know."

Murphy was relieved when, at last, the heavy wagon rolled slowly past several ancient cottonwood trees and through the large, timbered gates of the fort. He had never liked wagons, and the slow, monotonous trip had reinforced his dislike.

The fort matched the color of the brownish-red soil it was built upon. Everything, the exterior walls and the buildings inside, was constructed of unplastered adobe brick. A young Indian boy ran alongside the wagon dancing and yelling until the mules stopped beside a long rectangular building with a wooden porch extending from corner to corner. Then he was gone.

"COMMISSARY," Murphy read from the sign above the door. Further down, another sign hung from the porch roof: CANTEEN.

That's what I need, thought Murphy. A cool beer and some shade to drink it under. He placed his rifle and the Greener under the wagon seat and stepped down.

He was waiting on the veranda for Skeet, when the commissary door opened and a smartly dressed man in a brown suit backed out of the doorway onto the boardwalk.

A loud voice carried from inside. "Thank you, Mr. Gibson. We'll be looking forward to hearing from you again."

Gibson.

The name echoed through Murphy's brain as the man closed the door and turned, almost running into him. Murphy did not flinch or move. His voice was calm.

"Howdy. I'm Al Murphy."

Panic flooded Gibson's brown eyes and face. Murphy saw it—in that flickering instant before the meticulously groomed man regained his composure and half-smiled, he saw it.

"Ah, ah, Mr. Murphy." Gibson held out his right hand. "I don't believe I've had the pleasure."

Murphy glared coldly without raising his hand. "You're right, Mr. Gibson. You haven't had the pleasure. Some of your men have, though. I don't think they liked it. I don't think you'll like it either."

Skeet stepped beside Murphy, and Gibson used the opportunity to shift his eyes. "Hello, Skeet."

The skinny little man spit a stream of tobacco juice, most of which landed on Gibson's left boot. "Hello, yourself. Jerome Walker was a friend of mine."

Murphy smiled.

"I had nothing to do with that," Gibson said emphatically.

"Yeah, and you're a liar too," Skeet replied.

Gibson's eyes and manner changed. "You better be careful, little man."

"No," Murphy interrupted. "You're the one that had better be careful. I'm starting to get tired of your men. You'd be wise to call them off while you still have some left."

Gibson turned and walked briskly past the wagon into the open court.

"I guess I gave him what-for." Skeet said quietly.

"Yeah," Murphy grinned. "Who's this Walker fellow?"

"A mule skinner like me. Gibson's men killed him."

Murphy's smile left. "You'll be next, Skeet, if he can get it done. You spit on him and called him a liar. A man like him isn't use to that. He can't live with it."

They were silent. Each thinking. At length Murphy spoke. "Let's get a beer."

"Can't," Skeet said. "They'll unload the wagon for me, but I won't eat or drink till the mules are took care of."

Murphy grinned. "Guess you're right. I'll help you."

After unhitching, they led the mules to the post livery stables. Murphy was astonished at the size of the black man in denim overalls who met them in front. He had to be six-foot-six or better and weigh every bit of three hundred pounds.

"How do, Mr. Skeet. Let me help with them mules," the liveryman said.

"Howdy, Moses. I want for you to meet a friend of mine, Al Murphy."

The smallness of Skeet beside the man made him appear even bigger than before. Murphy extended his hand and felt it become lost in a huge hand that gently shook it.

"How do." The man smiled, with three missing front teeth.

"Fine," Murphy replied. "Nice to meet you."

Moses took the mules from Skeet. "Mr. Murphy, you just follow me with them mules."

In minutes, the mules were chewing contentedly on oat hay Moses provided them.

"Mr. Skeet. You want I should do the feet on them mules?"

"No, Moses. They're all right. Keep out plenty of hay. We'll be headin' out first light."

"Yessir, Mr. Skeet. I do it just that way."

Murphy watched Moses, carefully appraising him. He liked the big man. Even admired and respected him, all based on his own instinct, something Murphy did not understand but had learned to trust.

"Maybe I be seeing you again, Mr. Murphy."

"I hope so," he replied.

Skeet stepped beside Murphy. "Well?"

"Well, what? What does well mean?"

"It means you offered to buy me a beer."

"I don't remember offering to *buy* it." Murphy scratched his chin.

"Well, you did."

"All right, Skeet. Fine. I'll buy."

There were no windows in the canteen and it was much cooler than outside. Murphy and Skeet moved to a long bar. Two soldiers, cavalrymen dressed in blue garb, were farther down at the corner. Three other soldiers sat at a table located close to the open doorway, playing poker. They used the daylight from the door to see their cards.

"What'll it be?" A fat, bald man behind the bar asked.

"Beer," Murphy said.

They took the heavy clay mugs to a table and sat down. "How well do you know Moses, Skeet?"

"Ah, not that well, really. I see him every run, of course. What little I know, I heard it around. That's how come I won't let him shoe the mules."

"Why?"

"They say that one time a mule gave him trouble about his feet and kicked at him. It made Moses so mad he broke the mule's leg."

Skeet took a sip, then continued. "Can you think of that? How strong a man would have to be to break a mule or horse's hind leg?"

"I've heard of it," Murphy said. "But I never met the man who could do it, until now. What else do you know about him?"

"He was in the cavalry, but they kept him at the post all the time, so he got out. There wasn't no horses big enough to carry him for very long. Except for that, I don't know nothin' else—'cept I like him."

Murphy drank the warm beer, wishing it were cooler. He took the makings from his pocket and rolled a smoke. His thoughts turned to Christine, then to the sheriff. *I doubt if he's found anything to tie Gibson to Jake Mc-Cormick's murder,* he thought. *It probably wouldn't do him any good if he did. I'll have to tell him about the other night at the seep spring when I see him.*

Finishing the beer, Murphy stood and rubbed his face with his hand. "There a bathhouse around here? I think I'll shave and clean up a little."

"Sure. Two buildings down and behind the armory. They'll let you use it for nothin'," Skeet answered.

"A bath wouldn't hurt the smell of you either," Murphy said. "Better come with me."

"Naw, I don't need one, you go ahead. I'll be here when you're done."

Murphy smiled. "Come on, a little water won't hurt you."

"It won't help me none neither. You go on."

Outside, the sun was low in the west. A small detachment of soldiers rode through the gate, drawing Murphy's attention. It did not appear they had been gone long. Their clothes were fairly clean and the flanks of their horses were not drawn in like they would have been if they had traveled far. They had probably gone to the reservation that morning and now were back.

A kettle sat in a large fire pit in front of the pine hut that was the bathhouse. The fire was out and the place looked empty.

Murphy stepped into the small building. The floor was made of rough-sawn wooden planks, and the air smelled of wood rot and mildew. A square opening in the thatched brush roof provided a small amount of inside light.

Four ropes, evenly spaced, hung from the ceiling. He

took his clothes off and with the Smith in his right hand, pulled one of the ropes with his left.

A small wooden flume mounted on springs lowered, and a stream of water began to flow out. He laid the gun on a narrow shelf and stood in the water. It was cold, almost too cold. Hurriedly he rubbed his hair and body, washing without soap. The bandage on his side came loose and he inspected his wound. It looked better. The infection was gone and it was starting to heal.

Ten minutes later, he emerged from the bathhouse refreshed. I may not be much cleaner, he thought, but I sure feel better. Too bad there wasn't any hot water, soap, or a razor.

Murphy walked back toward the canteen in the hazy dusk light. The evening breeze felt good. He turned the corner of the armory and saw a group of men in front of the commissary—where the canteen was located.

He heard hard words.

"You still like to spit, old man. How do you like this?"

The slap of a fist striking flesh sounded sharp and clear.

Murphy moved before he heard anymore. He ran toward the group, the Smith in his hand.

He was fifteen yards from them when he saw four men suddenly tumble to the ground and Moses's tall frame standing above the others. Two men in the crowd went for their guns.

They'll kill him, Murphy thought. He pointed the gun and pulled the trigger. The Smith bucked in his hand and one man jerked sideways and went down. He pulled the trigger again, shooting double-action, and the other man shot his revolver into the ground twice before he fell backward.

Men were running, running away. Murphy leveled his gun on one man's back. He wanted to pull the trigger, to kill him, to kill them all.

"No, Mr. Murphy. No," Moses yelled.

A shot fired by one of the running men struck the dirt at Murphy's feet. He moved the Smith back and forth but could not find a target.

Then they were gone. Only Moses remained, kneeling beside a small man who lay unconscious.

It was Skeet.

# CHAPTER 7

AL MURPHY LAY on a bunk, in a cell, in the Fort Crosston stockade. And fate still held him.

Everything had happened so fast, maybe one minute total. Two men were dead. He had stood beside Moses. Skeet's battered body lay at their feet.

Seconds later, several soldiers encircled him, pointing their guns. They took the Smith from his holster and marched him to the jail while Moses pleaded with them for his release.

He lay there thinking, hoping Skeet would be all right.

A soldier came in and lit the single lantern that hung in the center of the hall separating the cells. Murphy looked at the light. His thoughts turned to all that had happened during the past week. Had it been only a week?

He reviewed the times he had used his gun. There were no regrets, no sympathy for the men he had killed.

Justified—he pronounced the sentence upon himself. "I wouldn't, I couldn't have done anything different," he whispered.

Metal clanged against metal. A soldier approached the cell. His uniform was neatly pressed and he had an air about him. The air of authority. It was evident in his movements and the way he held his tall frame.

"Murphy?"

Al sat up on the edge of the bed. "Yes."

"I'm Major Hilleary, commander of this post. Several men, witnesses to this evening's incident, have come into my office. All but one of them have testified that you killed two men without cause, that your act was murder."

The major removed his hat. "There will be a formal inquiry into the matter at ten o'clock tomorrow. You will have the opportunity to speak then. I'm here because I happen to know and trust the one man who claims you are innocent. He said you saved his life. I would like to hear your side of the story now, in an informal manner."

"How's Skeet?" Murphy asked.

"The medic has told me he is badly bruised and his nose and a few ribs are broken. He should recover in a few weeks."

Murphy saw the peril of the situation he faced. Gibson's men, no doubt under his direction, intended to use this fort and the law to do what they had been unable to. With enough witnesses, a court would have no choice but to find him guilty.

This man, this major, might be Murphy's only way out. His only hope. He thought about where his story should start. "Major, you might want to get a chair and a cup of coffee. This may take a while."

He started at the beginning, the day he rode the *grulla* from the west toward Turrett. Forty minutes passed before he finished the story, ending in the cell he now occupied.

The major stood. "I believe you. I have more reasons to believe you than you know, though I am not at liberty to discuss them. However, the situation is very ticklish. Eyewitness testimony will be difficult to dispute unless the witnesses' credibility can be destroyed."

The major paused a moment. "Tonight I will send a messenger to Turrett to report what has taken place here to the sheriff and to the mercantile. I will also ask the sheriff to check the seep-spring area you have mentioned and verify your account of what happened there."

Hilleary turned to leave, then changed his mind. "Mr. Murphy. This fort must be able to obtain supplies in order to carry out its mission. I was pleased when McCormick bid on the contract. Competition tends to create a better quality of merchandise at a reduced cost to the government."

The major stepped closer to Murphy's cell. "I cannot release you at this time, but know this: Any action which jeopardizes the success and maintenance of this fort concerns me. That includes the safe delivery of my supplies. I will do everything I can to insure justice is carried out in as swift a manner as possible."

The major left. Murphy lay back down on the cot, glad that he had told the man all he knew.

Justice. Would there be any? Could that many men be proven to be liars?

Murphy thought of Christine. It would hurt her to find out about Skeet. Would his situation affect her? He wondered for a time, before he fell asleep.

Sometime after midnight a voice woke him. "Mr. Murphy, Mr. Murphy. Wake up, Mr. Murphy."

Murphy recognized the voice. It was Moses. "What, what are you doing here?" he asked sleepily. He stood and looked out the barred window.

"I come to take you out of there. You got to come with me."

Big black hands wrapped around the bars.

"No, Moses. I can't leave like this. A major is supposed to help me. I'll be released in a few days. I'm sure of it."

"The major be a honest man. I know him. He say he'll help?"

"Yeah, he said he would. Now you get out of here before someone sees you."

"I ain't gonna be forgettin' what you done. Them men, they'd a kilt me for sure."

"We were both there to help Skeet. Now go on Moses, get away from here."

"I be back. They don't let you go, I be back for sure."

The hands left the bars. Murphy remained standing, gazing at the window above him. It was good. Good to have a friend. For too long he had shunned friendship, allowing no one to get close.

He knew Moses was grateful because he'd saved his life. The man would die if necessary to help him. But Moses had risked his own life to save Skeet, a man he barely knew. Murphy's throat tightened at the thought, and for a moment, a long-hidden soft spot in his heart controlled his emotions. He caught himself, stopped the thoughts, and lay down once again on the cot.

At dawn a soldier brought him breakfast. Biscuits covered with thick white gravy and a cup of coffee. Murphy did not feel like eating. He was nervous and had barely slept.

He was worried. Not for himself, but for Moses, Skeet, and Christine. Gibson hated Murphy and anyone who befriended him. So far, he was the only real problem Gibson had encountered in the implementation of his plans. And that problem may now be solved, Murphy thought, looking at the bars surrounding him.

Three hours later, three handcuffed men were led past his cell by four soldiers, two in back and two in front. The men would not look at him. They kept their eyes straight ahead. They were placed in the two cells farthest from his own.

Two of the soldiers, one with his army-issue Colt drawn, stopped beside Murphy's cell. "Time for your hearing."

They handcuffed him, and one soldier had started to place shackles on his ankles, when the other stopped him.

"No. The major said not to."

Outside the stockade, a few men stood several yards away. "Murderin' backshooter," one of them yelled. The others joined in, screaming obscenities.

Murphy paid no attention. His thoughts and his eyes were directed at one man who stood alone and to the side with a smirk on his face.

Gibson.

Murphy was taken to another building, south of the entry gate to the fort. A long sign hung above the steps leading to the veranda:

MAJOR R. J. HILLEARY, COMMANDER

Inside was a long hallway partitioned by adobe walls. Their footsteps sounded loud and hollow on the polished plank floor. They stopped at the end, and the lead soldier knocked on a door to the left.

The door opened. The room contained two rows of empty wooden benches. They sat Murphy down in a single chair in front, facing a platform with five men seated behind a long table. All officers, Murphy thought, judging by their neat appearance and dress uniforms.

Major Hilleary, who sat in the center, spoke. "Mr. Murphy, this inquiry is conducted to determine if sufficient evidence exists to schedule a court trial charging you with murder in the death of two men, James C. McMurry and Dan L. Black.

"We have heard testimony and received written affidavits from several witnesses to the incident yesterday evening. We now give you opportunity to speak in your behalf, if you wish."

"I would like to speak," Murphy responded.

The story was the same as the one he had told the major last night, except many details were omitted to shorten it. Twenty minutes later he finished.

"Mr. Murphy," the major said. "It will interest you to know that the freight driver you testified you ran to help has picked out two of his assailants from a line of men."

The major cleared his throat. "One other man has also been identified by another witness who also has testified on your behalf. These men were potential witnesses for the prosecution, but they have now been charged with aggravated assault and interfering in the official business of a civilian contractor whose duties are vital to the success of government interests."

Murphy grinned. He couldn't help it. He was amazed at what Hilleary had accomplished in such a short period of time. Gibson lost this one, he thought.

Major Hilleary stood. "This inquiry will recess for fifteen minutes. Guards, remove the prisoner from the courtroom."

Fifteen minutes later, Murphy was again seated in the chair.

"The defendant will rise," Hilleary said.

Murphy stood.

"This council has reviewed all facts relating to the charge against you. We believe the two fatal shots you fired yesterday evening from one .44 Smith and Wesson revolver were not fired in self-defense.

"But we also believe that if you had not fired those shots, two innocent men may have been killed, both of whom were conducting official government business on this post."

The major smiled. "This council does not believe sufficient evidence exists to schedule a court trial on the open charge of murder. Guards, remove the handcuffs. Mr. Murphy, you are free to proceed to the armory and retrieve your weapon. This hearing is adjourned."

At the armory, Murphy buckled his gun belt around his waist and loaded the Smith. Freedom was good. He was happy, but somehow the gun didn't fit with his feelings.

He found himself wishing he didn't need it. Wishing he would never need a gun again.

"Where would the infirmary be?" he asked the armory guard.

"It's in the commissary, in a back room."

On his way there, Murphy noted the freight wagon had been unloaded. He checked under the seat and found his rifle and the Greener still there. Gibson is not going to like having his men in the stockade, he thought. Skeet may need this.

The commissary clerk saw Murphy enter the building and his eyes followed the Greener in Murphy's hands. "How can I help you?"

"Looking for the infirmary."

"Yes." The clerk pointed to the right rear corner. "The entrance is over there."

Murphy opened the door without knocking. Skeet sat on the edge of the first of several empty beds positioned neatly in a row. Bandages were wrapped around his waist, nose, and forehead. He raised his head when Murphy closed the door.

"Moses said you was in jail."

"I was. How are you?"

"Couldn't be better. Ain't you got eyes? What kind of a fool question is that? Can't you see I'm all tore up from one end to the other?"

Murphy grinned. "I brought you a present. Never know when you might need it." He handed the Greener and the shells to Skeet. "It's loaded."

"Well?"

"Well, what?"

"Ain't you gonna tell me what happened and how come they let you out?"

"Major Hilleary helped me. You—and I guess it was Moses—identified the men who beat you. That helped a bunch too. Before that, those men were witnesses against me."

"I was afraid you weren't gettin' out of this one," Skeet said. "Moses told me what you done. We wouldn't of left you in there long."

Skeet reached for his shirt, pulled it on, and started to button it. "I guess we better get goin'."

"Going?" Murphy asked. "You're not going anywhere.

You need to stay here and rest. It will be a long time before you are able to do anything."

"Nope. I'm leavin'. Ain't no good-lookin' nurses here, anyhow. Get me my boots. They're in that closet over there," he said, pointing.

"Skeet, you're not able to drive a team of mules for three hours, let alone three days, in the hot sun."

"I ain't drivin'. You are. Now get my boots."

"No, you're not going."

Skeet pointed the Greener at Murphy's belly and pulled one hammer back. "Do you think I'd let you try an' drive them mules without me? I don't think you can even harness 'em. Nope. Now, for the last time, get me my boots."

Murphy was sure Skeet wouldn't really shoot. At least, he didn't think so, but the old man's eyes were wild looking.

"All right. Have it your way," Murphy said, going to the closet. "But don't you whine one time during the trip. And if you die, I'm not burying you. I'll let the buzzards have you, if they can find any meat on your skinny bones."

# CHAPTER 8

OVER AN HOUR later, with Moses' help, the team was hitched, a few canned goods loaded, and the wagon ready to leave. Skeet was not able to do anything except talk, and Murphy and Moses were tired of listening to his directions.

"Skeet," Murphy said. "I've listened to you all I'm going to. If you don't shut up, I'm leaving you."

"Well, I wouldn't have to talk if you weren't so blasted dumb."

"Shut up."

"Well . . ."

Moses picked Skeet up and sat him gently on the wagon seat. The move was obviously painful to Skeet. His breathing became harsh, and sweat beaded his face.

"Sorry, Mr. Skeet," Moses said, smiling. "I didn't see how else you was goin' to get up on that wagon."

"You just wait, the both of you. Soon as I heal up, you're gonna know what-for. Treatin' an old man like me this way. Why, you both ought to be ashamed of yourselves."

Murphy climbed into the seat, released the wagon brake, and took the heavy reins in his hands.

"That ain't the way you hold 'em. Don't you know nothin'? Have you been this dumb your whole life? Turn your hands over and run them reins between your first and second fingers. You gotta feel the mules."

Murphy was out of patience. He did not even try to follow Skeet's advice. He popped the reins. "Yah—yah."

The mules lunged into their collars, breaking into a run.

"Hold 'em back, you fool. Turn 'em."

Murphy pulled the right rein.

"No, no." Skeet yelled, trying to grab the reins. "Pull 'em both."

The mules came to a stop. Moses stood in front of them, gasping for breath, and holding the reins to the lead mules.

"That's it," Skeet said breathlessly, fighting the stabbing pain in his sides. "Hand me them reins."

Several soldiers, hearing the excitement, stood in the court. They laughed and pointed their fingers.

Skeet motioned Moses to the side and weakly snapped the reins. A tiny ripple traveled the eight-mule length, and the animals stepped forward in unison and began to turn to the right.

But how, Murphy thought. He didn't even move his hands. How'd they know to turn?

Murphy lowered the brim of his hat in embarrassment as the wagon traveled smoothly by the soldiers. After they were out the fort gates he raised his hat brim and looked at the little man beside him. A new feeling grew inside. A respect that had not been there before. Driving a team of mules was not as easy as it looked . . .

Miles went by in silence. It was unmercifully hot and Murphy worried about Skeet. Sweat had caused the bandage on his nose to come loose, and after trying to put it back in place several times, Skeet finally gave up and threw it away. The nose looked bad. It was swollen twice its normal size and deep purple in color.

"Skeet, you're right I don't know much about driving mules. Will you show me again? Maybe I can learn so you can lay in the back and rest."

The old man took a plug of tobacco from his pocket and bit off a piece. "Watch my hands. See how the reins slide and fit in 'em."

That was all he said. Thirty minutes later he handed over the reins. Murphy fumbled briefly with them until he thought he held them correctly.

"To stop, pull 'em both even to you. Don't jerk 'em. You won't need to turn, they know the road, but . . ."

Skeet bent over the side of the wagon with his arms clutching his stomach and vomited. Murphy gently pulled the mules up and set the brake. There was no shade of any kind in sight and it was at least three hours before sundown.

Murphy stood and put his hands on Skeet's shoulders. "Better lay down."

Several painful movements later, the little man lay in back. Murphy rigged a tarp to shade him. He did not like what he had done, afraid that the tarp would trap the hot air and create an oven, but maybe it was better than the sun.

Skeet spoke quietly. "To turn, just use your fingers. You got to feel the lead mules—and they got to feel you."

"Don't worry. I'll be careful with them," Murphy replied.

Skeet raised a hand. "It'll be after dark before you come to the red tank. You might miss it—but them mules won't. Let 'em have their head."

Murphy sat back in the seat and released the brake. He carefully threaded the reins in his hands until satisfied, allowed a little slack, then snapped them. The ripple he created was rough, jagged, nothing like when Skeet did it. Nonetheless, the mules responded and leaned into their work, much to Al's relief.

The mules plodded ahead and Murphy kept a slight tension on the reins. Miles later, he began to feel them. To know them. He closed his eyes and tried to guess when they were gathering their strength to pull through spots of sand or when the going was easy. Surprisingly, his guesses were often correct.

At last the sun started to disappear. He stopped the wagon and removed the tarp. Skeet's clothes, face, and hair were drenched in sweat. His skin was white. Too white.

"You're doin' fine," Skeet whispered. "I can tell."

"I knew you shouldn't have come. It was a mistake. I shouldn't have allowed it."

"Shut up." Skeet tried to smile.

Murphy unhooked the canteen from the side of the wagon, opened it, and put it to the old man's lips. "Drink all you can. I better keep moving."

Two hours or so after dark, the sound of the mules' hooves hitting the ground changed. Murphy knew they had left the hard-packed road and now traveled on soft ground. Must be close to the tank, he thought.

The mules soon stopped on their own. Murphy set the brake and stepped down. The night was so black he could not see Skeet in the wagon bed.

"How are you?" Murphy asked.

"Help me out." Skeet's voice was stronger than earlier. Murphy helped him crawl to the end of the wagon, then picked him up and set him on the ground, feet first. Skeet leaned weakly against the wagon side. "You sure don't weigh much," Murphy said. "You ought to eat more."

Skeet's breathing was short, choppy. "Leave me be and do the mules."

Murphy went about gathering what wood he could find for a fire. He needed some light to be able to unbuckle the harness from the mules. The mesquite bushes provided larger pieces than the greasewood. Thorns cut and poked his hands and arms as he searched for them. Finally he thought he had enough.

He was nursing a tiny flame, blowing gently into it, when he heard something in the direction from which they had come. Immediately he stamped the fire out and stood still, trying to hear the noise again.

One of the mules brayed and a horse answered, whinnying into the night stillness, hundreds of yards away. Murphy moved to Skeet. "We've got visitors," he said quietly. "You better get down and stay under the wagon. I'm going to meet whoever it is."

Out of habit, Murphy's hand checked his holster to ensure the Smith was in it. He left, walking swiftly toward the main road. Presently he saw a faint outline of ruts a few feet in front of him. He stopped to listen. Hooves thudded against the ground from somewhere below him. The sound was clear and became louder.

One of Gibson's spies, Murphy thought. If I call to him, stop him, I won't be able to see well enough to know if he goes for his gun.

The hooves moved closer. Only one thing to do, he thought. He stepped back from the road and crouched down. His heart beat rapidly.

A vague, fuzzy outline of a horse and rider came into view. Murphy sprang forward. Leaping through the air, he hit the rider with all the momentum he could muster.

A wall. It was like hitting a solid rock wall. Then Murphy was thrown forcefully to the ground. He landed on his wounded side and sharp pain shot to his brain.

An arm wrapped around his neck and throat stopping the air flow to his lungs. He grappled for the Smith. A hand quickly took his arm and held it in a steellike vise to the ground.

I'm going to die—the words raced through Murphy's mind. He gathered his strength for one last try—one final attempt to free himself.

Nothing. Complete futility. His effort did not even faze the man who held him. He thought his lungs would burst when the man spoke.

"You shouldn't a-scared me that way."

The voice. It could belong to only one man.

"Moses," Murphy cried out with all that was within him. The effort produced only a hoarse whisper, barely loud enough for the man to hear. The hold on his throat released and air rushed in. Sweet, wonderful, pure air.

"It's—it's me. Al—Mur—phy."

"That you, Mr. Murphy? I thought sure you was one of them bad mens. I be sorry, awful sorry. Let me help you to get up."

Murphy's breathing slowly became easier. He rubbed his neck, still shaken.

"Moses. What—what are you doing here?"

"I come to find you. But not this way. I surely didn't come to find you this way. I be sorry, Mr. Murphy. I didn't know who you was. I surely didn't."

"Why are you here?"

"I heard them men. They got their horses a while after you was gone. They talked your name and Mr. Skeet's. I come to tell you, to help you."

"How many were there? Was any of them wearing a suit?"

"Sure was. One of them was wearin' nice clothes, real nice. Some more, maybe five or six, was with him. They up to no good, them men. I was fearin' they was after you and Mr. Skeet. That's why I come to tell you."

Murphy scratched his throat. "Thanks, Moses—you know you almost killed me."

"Sorry 'bout that, Mr. Murphy."

"Moses, don't call me mister anymore. And quit saying you're sorry. None of this was your fault. I jumped you, and you did what you had to. Skeet is up with the wagon. We better go see about him."

"My horse. I got to find him. Maybe he done gone to the mules."

"That was your horse?"

"Sure was. He be big and strong. Took almost three months pay to buy him."

"Skeet," Murphy called, nearing the wagon.

"It's a good thing you yelled out," Skeet said, his voice surprisingly strong. "I was gettin' ready to blast you to pieces. Who was it?"

"You were supposed to sit under the wagon and rest," Murphy scolded.

"What do you think I'd do? You go off and leave me and expect me to just sit around waitin' all night in the dark."

"Moses is here with me."

"Moses? What in tarnation is he doing out here?"

"I'll tell you about it, but first I'm going to build a fire, unhook the mules, and make some coffee."

# CHAPTER 9

THE INFORMATION MOSES had provided about Gibson and his men worried Murphy as he set the pot of water and coffee grounds next to the fire. He saw Moses unhooking the mules in the firelight and walked to him. "Did you find your horse?"

"Sure did, Mr.—"

"I told you not to call me mister."

Moses smiled. "He was up there with them lead mules."

"After we water the stock and eat, we better pull out. It might be better to travel all night and rest in the day. Besides, it'll be easier on Skeet than the heat. I'll help you with the mules."

The coffee was about to boil over when Murphy and Moses finished watering the mules and returned. Skeet lay beside the fire, asleep. Murphy gently nudged Skeet's boot with his. "Wake up."

"What?" Skeet sat up and winced at the pain caused by the action.

"Coffee's ready, Mr. Skeet," Moses grinned. "You want some?"

"What kind of a fool question is that? Of course, I want some. Murphy, you said you was gonna tell me what happened. Well, ain't you?"

Murphy studied Skeet in the flickering light from the fire. He looked better, except his nose. Much of his color had returned and his eyes were not glassy like they had been earlier.

"Moses almost killed me," Murphy said.

"What'd you say? Moses almost killed you? That's the

**61**

craziest thing I ever heard of. Moses wouldn't kill nobody, let alone you. What kind of fool talk is that? I never heard of such a thing."

Eventually, while they ate crusty hard bread, jerky, and canned tomatoes, Murphy told the story. Finished with his coffee, he carefully rolled a cigarette. "I don't want to, but I guess we better hitch the mules and get moving. Moses, what's your plans?"

"I dunno. Guess I just head back to the fort."

"What are they payin' you there anyway?" Skeet asked.

"They pay me purty good. Twenty dollars a month and—"

"That ain't good," Skeet said. "You can make fifteen dollars a week drivin' mules if you come with us."

"What Skeet's telling you is true," Murphy said, "but he didn't mention you'd become a target for Gibson's men."

"That's nothin'," Skeet said testily. "That's what you been hired to tend to."

"Maybe not," Murphy said. "This may be my last trip."

"What do you mean your last trip? What are you talkin' about? Course you're gonna go on the next run. What's the—"

"Skeet," Murphy said sharply. "Drop it. I don't want to see Moses tangled up in things he need not be a part of. When we get back, I may travel on."

Soon the mules were hitched, the fire out, and Skeet lay in the wagon bed on some tarps. Moses threw his saddle in the wagon beside Skeet's feet and tied his big buckskin workhorse to the tailgate.

Murphy stepped beside him. "Moses, I appreciate you coming to warn us about Gibson, but there's no reason for you to get involved in this. Dead men can't spend money and there's more to this trouble than you know."

"I hears you, Mr.—ah, Murphy. Only I need the money. I got kinsfolk workin' for most nearly nothin' back home, an' I sure do like to help 'em. Maybe bring 'em out here where they can own their own land. They real good at farmin'."

Murphy paused, thinking. It really wasn't his decision. He knew that. But he had interfered because he did not want the big man to get hurt. Moses' strength and brawn were no match for bullets. At last he spoke. "All right, I guess it's something you have to do. I hope you're making the right choice and I wish you luck."

"Thanks, Murphy." He smiled.

Moses took the reins and started the reluctant mules forward. The night was pleasant and Murphy wondered how it could be so miserably hot, then so cool and nice, all in the same day.

And he thought about his life, and the situation he now found himself in. He felt detached and far away from everything. Events, happenings, but he had not really been a part of them.

He had only watched while another man, a man named Murphy had played his role.

There was no anger or hate inside of him now. I think I will, he thought. I'll leave when we get back. Maybe head north. A lot of country up there I haven't seen.

A picture came to his mind. A woman, the sunlight shining in her long blond hair. There was more, though Murphy did not understand it. Maybe it was the way Christine held her head or a kind of pride that revealed itself in her every movement. Whatever it was, he liked it.

The wagon rolled slowly through the night. At full daybreak they reached the seep springs. Murphy carefully searched the draw for any fresh tracks and then the salt cedars surrounding the water for anyone who might be hidden there, waiting in ambush. He found nothing.

Where could Gibson and his men have gone? Murphy thought. They can travel twice as fast on horseback as we can. They had to water their horses here on the way to

Turrett, especially if they passed up the dirt tank. Why haven't they hit us? What are they up to?

The puzzle continued to bother him while he searched the top of the low ridges above the draw for signs of the fight four nights ago, knowing that the heavy rain had probably wiped out the tracks.

There could be men though, dead men who are still here, he thought. The sheriff and Christine couldn't have received the message from Major Hilleary until last night, at the earliest. Laker hasn't had time to check the area yet, if he even decides to.

He searched the sky. No buzzards. I know several of my shots were on, he thought. They must have come back and carried their dead or wounded with them.

In several places he found boot imprints that had been made in mud. Whether they were made while it rained or afterward was impossible to tell. An object gleamed in a greasewood bush in front of him. He went to it and found a .44 Colt revolver, the same caliber as his Smith. The gun had begun to rust on the side that had been against the earth.

He found nothing else, and weariness made him go back to the wagon. The hobbled mules were grazing contentedly on various patches of sand grass while Moses' buckskin roamed freely among them. Skeet and Moses had made their beds on the west side of the wagon in the shade and were both asleep.

Fairly convinced that wherever Gibson was, he wouldn't be coming by the spring, Murphy quickly joined the sleeping men.

They rested the whole day, moving their beds every few hours to take advantage of the moving wagon shade. No one came to disturb them. A short time before nightfall, they pulled out once again on the last leg of the trip.

"We'll make it to Turrett easy before sunup," Skeet said

from the back of the wagon. "I kind of like this night goin'. It's easy on the mules."

"That the only reason?" Murphy chuckled. "Is it just the mules you're worried about?"

"Well, I like it, too. Is there somethin' wrong with that? Can't a man like what he wants to, when he wants to? That's the trouble with you young folks. You're always tryin' to make somethin' big out of nothin'. I just say somethin', one little thing, and you go an' try to make some big deal out of it. Why I remember when . . ."

The air was cool and sweet and the day's rest had invigorated Murphy. To break the boredom of the remainder of the trip, he decided to have some fun. "Skeet, you're feeling better, aren't you? I can tell because you won't shut your big mouth. I liked you better when you were too sick to talk. Then I didn't have to listen to you."

"You young pup! Who do you think you're talkin' to? Ain't you got no respect for your elders? You ought to be ashamed. If I was a few years younger I'd . . ."

And the miles wore on. Every time the conversation lulled, or Skeet sulked, Murphy thought of something to say to get him going again. Occasionally Moses even helped. They knew, even Skeet knew—in the back of his mind—that it was all just a game. A way to pass the time and nothing personal was intended in any of it.

Finally fatigue and monotony took over and ended the talking. The last hour or so into Turrett was in silence. They were glad when the wagon stopped in front of the mercantile. No lights shone from the windows.

"Wonder what time it is," Murphy said.

"It don't matter none," Skeet grunted. "Moses, help me to get out of here and I'll wake up that no-account clerk and make him get us some coffee boiling. You and Murphy tend to the mules."

After finishing their chore, Murphy and Moses followed the side of the building as Skeet had done and found a door beside a lighted window. Murphy opened it and quickly realized it wasn't a clerk Skeet had woke up, it was Christine.

"Be more careful, can't you see it hurts," Skeet was grumbling. She was busy putting salve on Skeet's nose and did not notice Murphy standing in the doorway.

"Quit cryin'," Murphy said.

Christine looked up. Seeing Murphy, she smiled. "I'm glad you're here. Come in and close the door."

"I've got a friend with me." Murphy moved over and Moses entered, his floppy brown hat in his hand. He had to bend down to keep from hitting his head on the top doorjamb.

Christine grabbed a towel and wiped her hands. She went to Moses and extended her right hand, trying to hide her surprise at the man's size. "I'm Christine McCormick."

Moses stared at her hand a moment.

"Something wrong?" she said.

"No, no, ma'am. How do," he said, taking her hand ever so gently. "I—I is Moses."

"You come in and sit down. The coffee will be ready in a minute, then I'll fix the three of you more breakfast than you can eat. After that we'll talk."

Skeet rose from the large plank table.

"Sit back down," she scolded. "I'm not through with you."

Her words about breakfast were true. Though Moses ate a mountain of food, there were still a few biscuits, some gravy, scrambled eggs, and salt pork left over.

"I thank you, ma'am," Moses said. "I never had a breakfast like this 'un. Not in my whole life." He rose from the table. "I do them dishes."

"You certainly will not. You sit back down." She filled his coffee cup.

"More coffee, Mr. Murphy?" she said.

"My name's Al, Miss McCormick. There's no mister on it," he said.

Her eyes met his evenly. "My name is Christine. And there's no Miss on it either."

They smiled. She filled his cup, sat down, and spoke. "A message came in from the fort telling me some of the things that happened to you and Skeet there. I started to leave the minute I received it, but the sheriff talked me into waiting another day or so until he or one of his deputies could go with me."

She took a breath. "Three nights ago someone set fire to Gibson's ranch and killed two of his men. We don't know who did it, but we think it was some of my ranch hands, seeking revenge for Jake's death. Gibson apparently was not there."

"Of course he wasn't there," interrupted Skeet. "He was down at the fort tryin' to kill me an' Murphy."

"Did they burn his house?" Murphy asked.

"Yes. I haven't seen it, but the talk around is that there is nothing left."

"Where is Gibson's ranch?"

"About twenty miles south of here."

"That's it," Murphy said. "Moses followed us to tell us that Gibson and his men left the fort a few hours after we did. We never saw them and they didn't water their horses at the seep spring. I couldn't figure out where they had gone or why they hadn't hit us. A messenger must have found Gibson and told him about his ranch. He must have gone to it instead of coming to Turrett."

Murphy took his tobacco sack from his pocket. "You know what this means. Now Gibson has to get even. Your ranch is next, or this store. This thing will go on and on until either you or Gibson is dead. Dozens of men will be killed and this town will be torn to pieces."

Christine sighed. "I know. I don't know what to do to

stop it except leave, run, let Gibson have everything. I can't do that. I won't do that."

"Then you better be prepared to fight, and fight hard," Murphy said solemnly. "You can't sit around waiting for his next move. You have to move, you have to take it to him with everything you've got."

She slumped back in her chair. "I hoped Laker would do something. If he would find and arrest Gibson, that would stop everything."

"Maybe," Murphy said slowly. "And maybe not."

"What about me?" Skeet interrupted. "Don't you want to hear what I done? I spit on Gibson's pretty black boots and called him a liar right to his face. And they jumped us at the seep spring, but we was ready for 'em. They won't be forgettin' what we done to 'em there.

"And me and Moses would have died for sure at the fort if it hadn't been for Murphy. He come up and killed two of 'em that was beatin' on me. And the soldiers arrested him. And what about Moses? He purty near killed Murphy."

"What?" Christine said.

"Well, he did. Don't you want to hear about us and what we done?"

"Yes I do, Skeet. One story at a time. Starting at the beginning."

# CHAPTER 10

THE MORNING SUN was high before the many stories had been told. Skeet and Moses had gone to the small company bunkhouse located behind the mercantile to sleep, leaving Murphy and Christine sitting at the table alone.

"You can't send another freight wagon out," Murphy said. "Gibson won't let it go through."

"I was counting on you to ride with it, in case there was trouble."

"No. That won't do. Putting me with a wagon increases the likelihood of it being hit, though I think it's a sure bet anyway. Besides, haulin' freight isn't something I want to do much of. I don't like it."

Murphy paused. Christine nodded her head and nervously fingered her coffee cup.

"Look," he said. "I'm only making things worse for you. Gibson has to get rid of me. He knows that. I think I'll make it easy for him. Maybe that way, at least some of the killing will stop."

She looked up. "What are you saying? What do you intend to do?"

He thought his mind was made up. Now, with her, he wasn't sure. The words came hard. "Guess I'll pull out. Maybe head north."

At once her manner changed. "Laker found out about some of your past, and your law experience. He told me about it. The great Al Murphy. I thought you were the one man who wouldn't run from anything or anyone. It looks like I was wrong."

Murphy stood. His chair screeched on the floor. The

69

hammer of the Colt he had found was tucked in his waist band and it poked him. He pulled it out. "None of this concerns me. I'm not running, and I don't care what you or anybody else thinks. I go where I want, when I want."

He threw the Colt on the table. "I found this at the seep springs. You can give it to the sheriff. It could help him, if he ever decides to do his job."

"Fifty dollars." She rose. "Fifty dollars a week and you won't have to go with the freight."

"That's all I am to you, isn't it—a hired gun? Well, not this time. You go and find another man. My guns are not for sale."

"Yes, they are." She put her hands on her hips. "You sold them in Cincherville and again in Fletcher!"

Her words infuriated him. Laker shouldn't have told her about Cincherville. Fletcher? What else did he tell her?

He started for the door. "That was different. That was the law."

"Al, wait," the tone of her voice changed. It lost its sharpness. He half turned. "The sheriff is basically a good man, but he's ready to retire. He knows he can't win a confrontation with Gibson. That's why he has been so reluctant to do anything. You are the only one here who is capable of standing up to Gibson, of stopping him."

She stepped toward him. "If you won't work for me, Laker could use a good deputy. I know he will hire you."

Murphy reached for the doorknob. "My lawman days are over. Good luck to you, and thanks for the breakfast."

He slammed the door behind him. He was confused. The decision to leave had been clear, even sensible in his mind. Now things were scrambled. He stopped on the edge of the street beside the front of the mercantile. No, he argued with himself. I'm leaving. She's not interested in me. All she wants is my help.

He turned and walked toward the livery. My horse ought to be in better shape, he thought.

Reaching a small corral behind the stable, he examined the *grulla*. The few days of plentiful feed and care had not changed the horse's appearance very much. His backbone and withers jutted out from his body, and the muscles in his shoulders and hips were easily defined because of the absence of any fat.

The *grulla* came to the fence, smelled Murphy's hands resting on the top rail, and snorted. It'll take a while, Murphy thought. I pulled him down too hard, went too many miles. He won't fully recover for weeks, maybe months.

And I'm leaving? How far can I go? What will I do when I get there, wherever there is?

He pulled some change from his front pants pocket and counted it. One dollar and eighty-five cents. Squeezing the money, he gazed into the corral without seeing it, thinking. I'm not crawling back and working for her for fifty dollars a week and I'm not going to be a deputy and fight her war for thirty dollars a month.

There was enough to buy a few cans of beans, a little coffee. He could get by for a few days. Maybe find a ranch not too far away that needed a hand and hole up there for a month or two until his horse was in better shape.

The decision made, he went into the livery stable, found his bridle, and returned to catch the *grulla*. He had just placed the bridle headband over the horse's ears when he heard the almost inaudible sound of footsteps behind him.

His move was involuntary. Automatic. He ducked low, whirled, and pulled the Smith in one blurred movement. The move startled the *grulla*, and he jumped several feet to the side, kicking up a shower of powdery dust.

Instantly Murphy leveled the gun and tightened his finger on the trigger, ready to fire double-action. Christine.

She stood by the corral fence, shaken by the suddenness

of his move, and the muzzle of the .44 pointing at her chest.

Murphy slowly lowered and holstered the gun. "I didn't know it was you."

"I can see that." Her voice trembled. "Who did you think it was?"

"I don't know. There's probably lots of people who wouldn't mind putting a bullet in my back. I'm not too partial to the idea."

"I—brought your rifle to you. It was in the wagon." He went to her and she handed it to him through the fence rails.

"Thanks."

"Your horse looks as if he could use more rest."

"Yeah, I guess so. But he's tough. He'll do all right."

There was a brief silence between them before she cleared her throat and spoke softly. "I want to apologize for the cruel things I said. You were right, none of this is your problem. You have already done more than anyone could possibly expect. Will you forgive me?"

"Yeah—well," Murphy extended his hand through the fence.

She shook it and withdrew her hand.

He started to turn and she stopped him. "Al, why don't you take your horse to my ranch and turn him out. The grass is plentiful. I'll see that no one rides him, and in a few months he won't look like the same animal."

A breeze blew her hair and she tucked it to the side. "I have over thirty horses on pasture, if they haven't been stolen. Take your pick. We can trade back if you ever come this way again."

Murphy did not answer immediately. The wheels in his mind turned rapidly. He believed she was sincere in what she had said, and he found himself not wanting to go.

At last he spoke. "I'll make you a deal. I'll put my horse on your place and pick out another one. Problem is, I don't want the *grulla* stolen. I'm no rancher, but for seventy-five dollars a month, I'll stay here, work your place, and try to hold the rustling down."

She answered without hesitation. "It's a deal."

"Good. One thing though. I'm my own boss, keep my own hours, and do it my own way. I'm not hiring out to do anything other than what we've agreed on here."

"Fine. I'll arrange for you to meet Ned, my foreman. I know he'll help you in any way he can. He has been like a brother to me. My father hired him when Ned was a youngster and he has been on the ranch ever since. Do you know where the ranch is?"

"Kind of. It's northwest of here, seven or eight miles, isn't it?"

"Yes."

A thought struck him. A pleasant thought. "You tied up at the store all day?"

"Yes, well—no, not really. I suppose I could leave it with the clerk. I usually stay close in case problems come up. Why do you ask?"

"I wondered if you might want to ride out with me and show me your place."

"I'd like that, but you must be terribly tired. You were up all last night. We can go tomorrow."

"No," he said. "I'm not hurting any. I'd rather go today. That way I can get another horse, come back into town tonight, and tomorrow gather the gear I'll need to stay out there for a while."

"All right, if you're sure. I'll meet you at the store in oh, say, half an hour?"

Murphy nodded. She turned and he watched her leave. He pondered what it was that made her so attractive to him. She was a beautiful woman, but that wasn't it. At least not all of it.

There were others who were equally pretty. Once again a picture of Midge came into his mind. Brown hair, straight and tied back, hanging from the rear of a droopy straw hat. Freckles—sun freckles that went across her nose, down her cheeks and neck, disappearing into the open throat of her dress.

He saw only one similarity between the two women. They both wore their hair long and straight. Midge had been just as pretty, if not prettier, in her own way. She was less formal and much easier to be around. I wish she were here, he thought. She understood things other women didn't.

Noise from the *grulla* broke his thoughts. The horse had stepped on a rein, pulling his head down, and he pawed the ground with his other hoof. Murphy went to him and pushed him backward by the bit and off the rein. He buckled the bridle throat latch. Guess I better get moving, he thought. I don't want to be late.

# CHAPTER 11

A SMALL, GOOD-LOOKING sorrel mare with a black-silver trimmed saddle and matching bridle stood tied to a hitching post in front of the mercantile when Murphy rode up. Christine came out of the store. She had changed into a tight-fitting tan blouse and a brown riding skirt.

"I'll bet that mare's yours," he said, pointing.

"Yes. Isn't she a doll? Jake bought her for me last spring." She began to unwrap the reins from the post, then stopped.

"Something wrong?" Murphy asked.

"No, no. It's nothing."

She finished unwrapping the reins.

"You sure you're okay?"

"Yes. It's—it's thinking about the mare. Jake gave her to me on my birthday. I miss him. I wish you could have known him."

She stepped beside her horse and handed Murphy a white envelope. "There is half a month's wages in advance. I thought you might need it."

"Thanks."

She swung into the saddle effortlessly and the mare began to dance, each hoof hardly touching the ground. Soon the town was behind them.

"I'm glad you asked me to show you the ranch," Christine said. "I like to ride. Lately there haven't been any opportunities."

"It'd be better if you didn't, not by yourself. Things aren't going to get any better. Gibson will strike back.

Maybe today, tonight, or tomorrow. It'll be soon. I wouldn't put it past him to kill a woman, or have her killed."

"What should I do?"

"Well, if I were you, I'd keep four or five men at the store and another four or five guarding the ranch house. Have them take shifts at night, and ensure at least one of them is always awake and watching."

"I'll do that," she said. "We'll tell Ned when we get to the ranch to split the men up."

"Not we. I'm giving advice because you asked for it. My job is only to keep the rustling down, remember?"

"I remember. But I don't understand. Three times Gibson has tried to kill you. That would make most men mad. Not you. You are determined to stay out of this and yet you are in the very heart of it."

"No, I'm not. I don't own anything and I don't have anything to lose, except my horse, and this job will help me look after him. I just happened along in time to be able to identify the men who killed your brother, so they tried to silence me."

"Doesn't it bother you that Gibson wants to kill you?"

"Look," he stopped the *grulla*. "I didn't take any trouble to Gibson's doorstep and I don't plan to. He brought it to me and it cost him.

"If he comes after me again, it will cost him more. But I'm only in this because of the fact that I am—was—broke."

She nodded angrily and spurred the mare. The horse jumped out of the road into a run.

The *grulla* wanted to run across the open flat with the mare, but Murphy held him in. What was that all about? he wondered. Why did she get so angry?

He gave the horse his head until he was in a slow, easy lope, then he checked him. Crossing the grama grass flat and entering a stand of cedar, he saw Christine on a narrow trail ahead, walking her mare. He urged the *grulla* on until he caught up with her.

"This trail go to the ranch?" he asked.

"Yes." Her voice was even. "It's a shortcut. The road to the ranch turns off of the main road about two miles west of here."

Murphy looked at the sun. Around noon, he thought. We should be there in about an hour. The trail began a gradual ascent up a long brushy ridge. He studied the terrain, painstakingly creating a mental map, one that he could trust to guide him even in the dark.

Christine stopped the mare. "Rattler," she said calmly. She dismounted and found a large rock.

"I can shoot it," Murphy said, stepping from the *grulla*.

She didn't answer. He moved to the front of the mare in time to see her heave a rock with both hands onto the snake's head.

"Guess I'm too late."

She moved past him, mounted, and clucked the mare forward without speaking.

Murphy smiled. Midge would have done that. She would have done it just that way, without saying a word. He swung in the saddle and the *grulla* snorted and shied sideways as they passed the still-thrashing length of snake.

The climb grew steeper and the trail began to zigzag. He had to shield his face frequently with his right arm and duck from the many branches sticking out into the trail. Soon the horses topped the bluff and a gentle wind met them.

Murphy gaped at the scene before him. The land lay flat for miles with lush grama grass reaching to a horse's shoulders. About fifteen miles to the north lay another mountain range, blue in the distance with sharp, jagged peaks. To the east and west he saw nothing. An endless expanse of grassy sea mixed with a sparse scattering of cedar.

"Christine." He stopped his horse. "Is this your place? Is this part of your ranch?"

She stopped the mare. "Yes. It's lovely, isn't it? I've seen this view thousands of times and it never ceases to overwhelm me. I've never been anywhere I thought was more beautiful. Sarah—Jake's widow—took the kids back East a couple of days ago. I don't blame her for leaving, but I'm going to stay and fight. This is my home."

Murphy nudged the *grulla* closer to her. "I'm beginning to understand. If I owned this, I wouldn't be too anxious to give it up either."

"It's not just the land, and especially not the store," she said. "If it were, I would give it up. It's what my father, my mother, and now Jake gave for it. For years, when I was small, we lived in constant dread of the Apaches. Turrett wasn't a town then. It was one trading post owned by a man named Ross Turrett. My father and mother fought for the right to be here. Now I must fight for the right to stay here."

She paused. "If only Jake were here."

"What happened to your folks?" Murphy asked.

"Four years ago rustlers came through and stole forty head of cattle. My father and Jake found their tracks and followed them. There was a fight and my father was wounded. He and Jake won and brought the cattle home, but the wound became infected and a few weeks later gangrene killed him."

She turned her head away from Murphy and spoke with a faint voice. "My mother couldn't live with his death. She sat in her room alone, week after week. Months passed. She wouldn't eat. One morning I found her, his picture in her hands."

She wiped her eyes with her sleeve.

"I'm sorry," Murphy said. "About your folks—about Jake."

Christine touched the mare with her small rowled spurs.

For several minutes they were both quiet, the sound of the horses' hooves lost in the rustling of the grass and the wind.

A raven circled above in the clear sky. The sound from the bird was forlorn and somehow seemed to match the story Christine had told and the serenity of the open plain.

Christine spoke, trying to make her voice as cheerful as possible. "It's a beautiful day. So what about you? What brought you to Turrett?"

"I don't know. I really don't. Just lucky, I guess," he smiled. "Seems I've been unlucky my whole life. Trouble has never been far from me. I wish it weren't that way. Once, for a short time, I had another life. A gentle life. Trouble took that away, too."

"Why did you quit working for the law? From what Laker told me, you had quite a reputation."

"It was no good. Things change. I became a drunk. The time came to leave, to leave everything. None of it mattered—not anymore."

"Were you ever married?"

"Once . . ."

"Was that the time you mentioned, the time when you had another life, a gentle life?"

"Yeah."

A herd of antelope ran from the side and crossed a few hundred yards in front of them. Murphy used the opportunity to change the subject. "Antelope sure can run, can't they?"

"Yes. When I was younger, I'd pick the fastest horse on the ranch and chase them. I never even came close."

"How come I haven't seen any cattle?"

"They're up there," she pointed at the mountains to the north. "On the summer range. In the winter we push them back here."

"Your range goes that far?"

"Farther. Though we don't use the country on the other side anymore. We don't have near as many cattle as we did before my father passed away."

Murphy relaxed his tired back and closed his eyes. The wind stung them and the lack of sleep unexpectedly became evident in his body. He opened his eyes and saw a slight depression in the land and the roofs of several structures that seconds earlier had not been visible.

The mare started to trot, her head held high. The *grulla* followed suit and in minutes they were there.

A windmill was situated in the middle of the ranch complex, pumping water into a wooden storage tank mounted on timbers. The tank was full and the overflow drained from a wooden flume into a large dirt holding tank. Two horses, one white and one a flea-bitten gray, whinnied from the tank and trotted to meet them.

They passed the tank and stopped their horses beside a hitching rail in front of the house. Murphy surveyed the surroundings. The place looked prosperous without being showy.

A bunkhouse and two sheds behind him with adjoining corrals were built of adobe with sod roofs. A large two-story barn, the bottom half adobe and the top made of rough-sawn planks, stood sixty yards to his left.

Only the house showed any signs of wealth. It was sizable, with plastered white walls and an ornately decorated wooden veranda that completely surrounded it.

A hatless man with a long white scruffy beard approached them from one of the sheds.

"Hi, Charley. This is Al Murphy." Christine said.

Murphy dismounted and shook the man's hand.

"I've heard of you," the old man said. "Most everybody has."

"Al will be spending a lot of time on the ranch, Charley. He'll be working to stop Gibson from stealing what cattle and horses we have left."

Charley looked at Murphy. "You're fixin' to be a might busy then, and you best get started. They's cattle bein' run off right now."

Christine swung lightly to the ground. "What are you talking about, Charley? Where's Ned?"

"He ain't here. One of the boys was ridin' the Turkey Creek country early this mornin' and run across seven or eight men drivin' a bunch of our cattle. He knew he couldn't stop 'em alone so he hurried back here. Ned and four men that was here went after 'em."

Christine sighed. "Is it ever going to stop?"

Murphy looked behind and pointed at the broad-chested, muscular gray horse that had followed the *grulla* from the tank. "If it's all right with you, Christine, I'll ride the gray."

"Yes . . ." She hesitated.

"Something wrong?"

"You can't have that horse, mister," Charley said. "That's Jake's horse."

"Yes, yes, take him," Christine said. "You'll—you'll need a horse like him. Jake said there was none better."

"I'll find another one I like," Murphy said.

"No, take him. I want you to. Jake is gone. He would want you to use the horse."

Murphy loosened the latigo strap on the *grulla* and began taking the saddle off. "Will you see if you can find me some foodstuff to take? I better get started."

"Get started? You can't leave, not now. You haven't had any sleep in almost two days and besides, you don't know the country. You couldn't find them."

"Now is as good a time as any to learn. Charley here is going to draw me a map and brief me while you get the grub ready. Aren't you, Charley?" Murphy turned to the old man.

"Yep. I can get you to where you can get around enough to get by. I can do that much."

"Good," Murphy said. "I'm good at getting by."

# CHAPTER 12

THE BIG GRAY was everything the *grulla* had been—months ago. He rode smooth, had a light, responsive mouth, and seemed to be tireless. Jake knew horses, Murphy thought, putting the horse into a long easy lope.

Murphy checked his shirt pocket for the map he and Charley had put together, though he didn't think he would need it. Every line and the directions he had heard were firmly established in his mind—including the location of Gibson's ranch, some twenty-seven miles to the south.

Strangely, Murphy no longer felt tired. The gray was full of energy and constantly dropped his head against the bit and reins to try to gain enough slack in them to run. Murphy softly jerked the horse's mouth in punishment and continued to hold a slight pressure.

To allow the horse to run now might mean he would have to walk later. The powerful horse's strength had to be maintained. The ride, Murphy knew, could easily last all night.

Two miles to the north the horse had not changed his gait. The wind grew steadily stronger and at times, when a burst hit, Murphy had to hold his hat to keep it from blowing off.

Seeing a small knoll ahead with a reddish-yellow rocky outcrop rimming it, he pulled the gray into a walk. Must be the hill Charley mentioned, he thought. From here, I should find their tracks less than three miles to the west and a little north.

He spurred the horse into a trot up the knoll. On top it seemed he could see forever. He looked in the direction he thought Turkey Creek should be and saw several brushy green draws in the distance that joined together at the end, forming a valley.

That must be the country, he thought. The wind became even more forceful and carried a hint of rain. He looked toward the east. Clouds, dark storm clouds, gathered the length of the horizon.

I better get moving, he thought. If that storm hits, there won't be any tracks left to follow. He allowed the gray to pick his way down the slope and then nudged him back into the same distance-eating lope as before.

Tall grass brushed Murphy's stirrups, and twice, hidden cactuses stuck needles in his boots. The gray stumbled occasionally, either stepping into a gopher hole or tripping on a clump of grass.

The land in front of him was deceptive. Although it appeared to be flat and endless, he found himself swallowed by depressions within the earth, unable to see more than a few hundred yards.

Armies could hide here, he thought, riding through one of the ancient lake beds.

A few patches of cedar began to appear, and Murphy reined the horse into a walk. Sweat lathered the gray's chest and the horse's breathing was loud from the five miles of nonstop galloping.

Murphy studied the waves of windblown grass, looking for a place where the grass had been trampled down by the hooves of cattle and horses.

Farther on, he climbed higher in elevation and the ground became rocky. Cedars became increasingly abundant, and the thick grama grass of the plains became short and patchy.

A buck mule deer with large antlers in the velvet jumped from its bed under a tree fifteen yards from him. The deer spooked the gray: the horse jumped four feet sideways and bolted. Murphy almost lost his seat in the saddle before stopping the horse. The gray snorted and pawed the ground.

I better turn south, Murphy thought. Go about a mile and then cut west until I find the creek. If I haven't found cattle tracks by then, I'll turn back north until I cross them.

A half mile south he found the tracks. He couldn't miss them. The ground was churned to powder where a group of tightly banded cattle had run.

A gale struck, and he quickly pushed his hat down tighter. Clouds drifted, shading the land, and Murphy looked east. The storm was closer. It'll be here in an hour or so, he thought.

He spurred the horse and again held him in the same gait as before. As he climbed the third ridge, muffled sounds reached him. He stopped the horse on top of the ridge and listened.

Again and again the sound came.

Shots?

The wind howled. He could not be sure. A cramped, tense feeling grew in his chest. He spurred the big horse into a run, giving him full rein. The cattle trail was plain, and the gray quickly began to follow it.

Across one draw and in the bottom of the next Murphy saw cattle running, mixed with a spatter of mounted men. The shots were clear now. Faster he spurred the gray. He pulled the Smith and a thought struck him. Ned, the foreman, and Christine's men don't know me. They may mistake me for one of the rustlers. I could be shot by the people I'm trying to help.

Several men moved into a group, running their horses in front of the cattle. Murphy turned the gray off the trail and angled along the side of the ridge toward them.

A tree limb caught his left shoulder and knocked him half out of the saddle. He regained his balance and the horse never missed a step, continuing to dodge the numerous trees and rocks.

He was almost to the bottom, sixty yards from the lead rustlers, when they saw him come from nowhere.

They turned in their saddles to shoot. Murphy fired double-action and missed. He cocked the hammer, shot again, and the rider closest to him clutched his stomach and fell from his horse.

Bullets whistled past Murphy. He knew he was in a bad position, between the rustlers in front and Christine's ranch hands behind. He emptied the Smith on the cattle thieves, firing double-action as fast as he could pull the trigger and not knowing if any of his shots were effective.

He pulled the gray to a sliding halt with his left hand while holstering the pistol, then grabbed the butt of his rifle. He jumped, pulling the long gun from its scabbard with the weight of his body.

Sharp pain from his old hip wound struck him. He ignored it and sat down. He levered the rifle and aligned the sights on the back of a rider now two hundred yards away.

His finger tightened on the trigger. He knew he would kill the man, that with a touch more finger pressure the .45–70 would leap in his hands and the man would fall.

Why he lowered the muzzle of the gun and carefully let the hammer down with his thumb, he did not know. He did not understand that the move was a dividing point in his life—the difference between killing because he wanted to and because he had to.

And the line between the two was sometimes thin, very thin.

He watched the ranch riders move by in chase, shooting now and then. The cattle had been left behind, and he saw them begin to mill and bawl.

Murphy scanned the area for the gray horse but did not see him. He rose and walked to the man he had shot. The man lay holding his guts, groaning. Murphy recognized him. He was the same small mustached man he had met the day he rode the *grulla* toward Turrett.

Fear filled the man's eyes at the sight of Murphy. "You," he yelled out and jerked his hand to his empty holster.

Murphy knelt beside him and moved the man's other hand away from the gunshot wound. It was bad. The bullet had entered a few inches from the side and torn through the guts, exiting the other side. There was little blood. A greenish yellow fluid trickled from the wound and the stench of bile and gas entered Murphy's nostrils. There was no hope. Nothing to do. The man would die.

It would be a slow, agonizing death, Murphy knew. He had seen it in the Indian Wars. Seen the belly swell to enormous proportions and the gangrene set in. Sometimes days would pass, and still death would not come to the strong young men.

Murphy's mind went blank. He stood and pulled the Smith, ejected the hulls, and loaded it. He did not think. He knew he must not think. Must not know what he was about to do or remember it afterward.

He cocked the gun and pointed the muzzle at the man's head.

"My God," the man cried out.

The report of the shot seemed to echo in Murphy's ears for hours before he turned from what he had done and walked slowly away. Thoughts, pictures from the past, tried to flood through the dam he created in his mind. The dam held and his mind remained blank.

Two men rode up to him, one leading the gray horse. They broke his self-imposed trance.

"Who are you? What are you doing with Jake Mc-Cormick's horse?" A middle-aged, straw-haired man asked.

"Murphy. Al Murphy. Christine loaned me the horse. Who are you?"

The man's eyes shifted nervously under Murphy's glare. "Name's Ned. I'm foreman of the Slash M."

Ned did not offer to shake hands, and there was an awkward tension between them. Intuitively Murphy disliked him, did not trust him. He wondered why Christine had spoken so highly of the man. He stepped forward and took the gray. "Thanks for catching the horse."

There was no reply, and Murphy shoved his rifle in the off-side scabbard and tightened the cinch. He mounted and the man who rode with Ned spoke. "We heard a shot a minute ago."

"One of Gibson's men is over there," Murphy pointed to the side. "He was gut-shot."

Murphy wheeled the gray and put his spurs to him, glad to be going, to be leaving what lay behind.

# CHAPTER 13

MUD IN THE main street of Turrett squished and splashed under the gray's plodding hooves. Murphy sat in the saddle, his head down and shoulders hunched forward.

The vicious storm had struck not long after he left Ned. He should have sought refuge from it and rested; he knew that now. Instead he had ridden through the brunt of it, hoping to reach Turrett by midnight. In the morning he intended to buy supplies and go back to the ranch to stay with the cattle.

Whiskey, he thought. A plate of hot food and a bed. He reached in his left saddlebag and felt in the sugar sack Christine had used to pack his food. The sack and its contents were soaked. He pulled his hand out and wiped biscuit dough from his fingers onto his pants.

It was late, though Murphy did not know the time. The town was quiet. The saloon lights were on and the door open. Four horses stood tied to a long hitching rail in front. Wearily he stepped from the gray, wrapped the reins around the rail three times, and loosened the cinch.

Inside, four men were at a table playing cards. Two others leaned against the bar. Murphy paid no attention to them, his thoughts fixed on the effect that first long drink would have on his mind and body.

"A bottle," Murphy told the barkeep, handing him a bill from the envelope Christine had given him. "Do you have any food? Hot food?"

"Beans is all that's left, but they're hot."

Murphy ignored the shot glass the bartender provided. He took the bottle to a table in the corner, sat down, and took a long pull of the hot, stinging liquid. Then another and another.

A plate of beans was set before him with a chunk of bread. Food never tasted so good, he thought, the whiskey quickly warming his belly and numbing his brain.

Murphy's attention did not shift from his dinner, and he did not notice the men at the table who watched him. A chair grated the floor in front of him and he looked up.

Gibson.

Murphy tried to hide his surprise. He shifted his eyes back to his plate and continued eating. The saloon was unnaturally quiet. The others, Murphy thought. They're with Gibson. If they intend to kill me, they may get it done tonight.

Strangely, the knowledge did not disturb him. He was too tired to care.

"May I sit down?" Gibson asked.

Murphy looked up with bloodshot eyes and nodded.

Gibson sat down. Murphy raised the bottle to his lips and drank. The whiskey went down smoother than before.

Gibson turned in his chair and snapped his fingers at the bartender. He then turned back to Murphy. "I understand you have been hired by Miss McCormick to protect her livestock?"

How could he know that? Murphy thought. By now he knows about the cattle, that his rustling attempt had failed. But the fact that I was there is not enough for him to make a statement like that. Someone told him.

Murphy continued to eat without speaking. A bottle and two glasses were set in front of Gibson. Gibson filled the two glasses and pushed one beside Murphy's plate. "You'll find that is a much finer bourbon than what you are accustomed to."

Murphy shoved the drink to the middle of the table, spilling half of it. "My whiskey suits me."

"I would like to make a proposition that I feel would be lucrative for both of us. Will you listen?"

Murphy swallowed. "I can hear."

"I'm sure you have heard a great deal about me and that my character is questionable. However, you must be careful not to form opinions based on information that is incorrect."

"It's correct," Murphy said. "Bullets don't lie."

"Of course there have been a few unfortunate incidents," Gibson smiled. "None of which were directed at you personally."

Murphy scowled. "Sure. I knew when the rope fell from my back and a bullet went through my side that no one meant anything by it. And when my bedroll was shot to pieces, I knew that was just an accident. They were aiming for somebody else."

The smile left Gibson's face. "I was here first. I built my mercantile first. There is not enough business in this county for two stores. One of us must close and it will not be me."

Gibson raised his left hand and moved the other to his coat lapel. "Allow me," he said.

Murphy nodded.

Gibson grasped an envelope with his fingers and placed it on the table. "There is one thousand dollars," he said in a low tone. "To earn it, all you must do is finish your dinner and ride out of Turrett. Leave and never come back."

The offer was tempting. A thousand dollars was more money than Murphy had seen in his life. It would buy a small place, a place he could live out his days in peace and solitude.

Murphy moved his elbow, and a spoon by the edge of the table fell to the floor. He bent to retrieve it and came up with the Smith in his hand. He cocked it and pointed the muzzle between Gibson's eyes.

The move was too fast. Too unexpected. Gibson's men had no time to react.

"Now," Murphy said. "I have a proposition for you. Take your money and get out of my sight or your brains will be splattered over half this saloon."

Gibson reached for the envelope with a hand that shook violently. He grasped it and stood. "I'll—I'll . . ."

"You'll what?" Murphy asked coolly.

Gibson turned and walked hurriedly from the saloon. The three other men at the table rose and followed him. The two at the bar turned to their drinks. Murphy laid the Smith on the table and took a drink.

Finished with the beans, he rolled a cigarette. I'm a fool, he thought. I should have taken the money, should have left. Why didn't I?

A picture of Christine came to his mind. It bothered him. Was she the reason?

He lit a match and moved it to his smoke. If she's the reason, he thought, the only reason, then I'm a double fool.

Murphy put the Smith in his holster and stood. The action caused a dizziness and he waited for it to clear before taking the bottle and walking to the saloon door. He stopped before exiting. Gibson may be outside, he thought. Waiting, waiting to get me.

He looked at the hitching rail. The gray stood quietly. The other horses were gone.

He thought of using the back door and sneaking around the building until he could determine whether an ambush had been set up for him. The thought rankled him. I'm not hiding from nobody. Gibson wants more trouble, he'll get it.

Without further thought, he crouched low and ran though the door. The whiskey had affected him more than he realized and he stumbled on the boardwalk edge, falling headlong into the muddy street. Shots rang out and bullets followed his sliding body, hitting the mud beside him.

Murphy's reflexes were dull and slow. He heard a bullet thud heavily into something to his left. He turned his head and through mud-covered eyes caught a glimpse of the big gray horse falling to his knees.

*Move*, his brain screamed to his arms and legs. He turned and saw the boardwalk in the light coming from the open saloon door. He scrambled and slid under it. Something struck his head. The report of gunshots continued for a moment. Then blackness. Nothingness.

# CHAPTER 14

MURPHY HEARD SINGING. It was pleasant, with a single deep voice.

> *Oh, the glory, oh the glory,*
> *that will be mine.*
> *When he comes . . .*

Murphy slowly opened his eyes and the singing stopped.

"Miss Christine, he waked up."

Murphy focused his eyes on Moses, who was standing beside him, smiling. He looked around and saw that he was in a room, in a bed. He raised himself up and a terrific pain exploded in his head. He closed his eyes and felt a hand push his chest down while another held the back of his head.

"Lie down. You mustn't try to get up." The woman's voice was soothing, reassuring, and the pain dimmed somewhat when he rested back on the pillow. He opened his eyes. Christine's face was close to his.

"Lie back and rest," she said. She took a towel and wiped beads of sweat from his forehead.

"Where—how—the gray, the gray," he said weakly.

"Shh . . . don't talk. Drink this."

The water soothed his throat, and his thoughts became more organized.

"You're here at the store," she continued. "You'll be fine in a few days."

"The gray?" Murphy's voice was a little stronger.

"Don't worry. There are lots of horses."

Murphy raised his hand to his hair and felt a bandage. He looked at Christine, his eyes asking the question.

"A bullet grazed the side of your skull. It's nothing serious."

"Gib—Gibson," Murphy said.

"We know. Two witnesses told the sheriff what happened. Now get some rest."

She backed away from the bed. He fought to keep his thoughts and his eyes open, but lost and fell back in a deep sleep.

"Moses," Christine whispered, motioning with her hand for him to follow. Outside the room, she closed the door. "I want you to find Skeet and . . ."

A knock sounded at the door. She opened it. "Come in, Sheriff."

"Thanks." He removed his hat and entered. "How's Murphy?"

"I think he'll be fine. He awoke a few minutes ago. He's very weak and he went back to sleep."

"I'm glad. Glad he came to. Sometimes they don't, not after two days and with a furrow in their head as deep as that one. He's lucky to be alive."

"Come, sit down," Christine said, going to the kitchen table.

Laker put his hand on Moses' shoulder. "You doing all right?"

"Sure am."

Laker moved to the table and sat down. Christine put a cup of hot coffee in front of him and said, "You look tired."

"I am." He took a sip. "I stayed up last night, waitin' to see if Gibson would come back into town. I intended to arrest him if he did."

The sheriff lowered his head and looked at the table. "One of your hands came into town early this mornin' before light. He told me a line shack of yours was burned last night and two of your men killed. The cowboy wanted to wake you up and tell you, but I told him I'd let you know later."

Christine shuddered, fighting anger, then stood suddenly and went to a cabinet. She returned, holding a small silver-plated Colt with ivory grips. "If you won't stop him, I will. I'll kill Gibson. I swear, I'll kill him!"

Laker rose and grabbed her arm. "No. He's not at his store anyway. Let me handle it."

"Let *you* handle it! Everyone in this county will be dead before you handle anything."

"Look," Laker said. "The judge has given me a warrant for Gibson's arrest. I've notified the marshal's office at Datil and requested help. I'm doing everything I can. I'll find him—and his men."

She jerked her arm from Laker's grasp. "When? For weeks you had every opportunity, and all you did was say you didn't have enough proof."

She moved to the kitchen counter and looked out the window. Moses stepped beside her. "Don't worry, Miss Christine. The sheriff will get them men."

"No, he won't. He'll do what he's been doing. Absolutely nothing."

"Take care of her, Moses," Laker said. "I'm down to one deputy. I've got to try to find some men."

"Make me a deputy. I sure can help to get them men."

"No, Moses. Thanks anyway. You're needed here."

After Laker left, Christine turned to Moses and said, "Find Skeet. Tell him to ride out to the ranch and tell Ned I want him to take me to Fort Crosston immediately."

She paused a moment. "And tell him not to tell anyone I'm leaving."

"Yes, ma'am."

Moses left and Christine readied a pack for the trip. She hurriedly changed into her riding clothes, knowing it would be at least four hours before Ned could possibly arrive. She was about to check on Murphy when she heard a voice outside and a knock at the door.

"It's me, Miss Christine."

"Come in, Moses."

He entered the room, hat in hand, and closed the door.

"Did you find Skeet?" she asked.

"Yes, m'am. He be on his way."

"Fine. Will you give my mare a double portion of grain? We'll be making a fast trip and she'll need it."

He started to leave.

"Then get some rest, Moses. You were up most of last night. I'll watch Al for a few hours before I leave."

"I be in the bunkhouse if you need me."

Moses left and Christine went into the room where Murphy lay asleep. He had not changed his position since she left him. She sat in a chair beside the bed and lowered her face into her hands.

Three hours later, she still had not moved as a gray hint of setting sunlight came through the bedroom windows. A knock came at the door and she found Ned and Skeet outside.

"Hi, Ned." She briefly hugged him. "Skeet, saddle my mare. We'll be leaving right away."

"How come I don't never get no hug. You don't even say hello to me. Just 'Skeet, saddle my mare.' Well, I done got her ready. She's in front of the store and I've a mind to go turn her loose."

"I'm sorry, Skeet. Come in, both of you, while I get my things."

Inside, Ned questioned her. "What's this all about? I heard Al Murphy is staying here?"

She turned to him. "Yes. You haven't met him yet, have you?"

"We've met." His voice was curt and harsh.

"Have you heard about the burning of the south line shack and the death of two of our men?"

"Ah, yeah. I—I heard about it. Why do you want to go to the fort?" Ned asked.

"The sheriff won't catch Gibson. Even if he did, Gibson would kill him. Major Hilleary is counting on a delivery of supplies and there is no way Gibson is going to allow us to freight them. I need the major's help and I'm going to the fort to plead with him to send soldiers to accompany the wagons and guard the store."

"It's a civilian matter," Ned replied. "The major won't help, and I don't think he needs to be involved."

Christine took her pack from the table. "Al, I mean Mr. Murphy, told me the major said the supplies were important and he would do whatever is necessary to see that he received them."

Ned hesitated, then spoke. "Why not let me go alone? I'll talk to the major. It'll be a hard, fast trip, and besides, you need to stay here and look after the store."

"No, everything depends on his decision. I must talk with him."

"You don't trust me?" Ned asked.

"Of course I do. You've been with the family a long time. But this is very important and I believe the major may be more willing to help if I speak with him in person."

"I'm goin' too," Skeet interrupted.

"No," Christine said. "I need you and Moses to stay here and take care of the store. And Mr. Murphy."

Skeet was annoyed. "Moses and that sorry clerk of yours can watch the store. I don't see why     "

"Skeet," she said sharply.

"Well, okay. But you're liable to wish you had me and the Greener. That's for sure."

# CHAPTER 15

MURPHY STIRRED IN the bed. The odor of burning wood was strong in his nostrils. His subconscious told him to ignore it, that it was part of a dream, but his senses cried out for him to wake.

The stench entered his mouth and throat. He could taste it. He coughed and the action caused a piercing pain in his head.

He opened his eyes. The room was dark. His thoughts were jumbled. Smoke, he thought. Gradually his mind began to clear and the thought came.

Fire.

He started to rise from the bed, but pain throbbed in his brain and he lay back down. I have to, he thought. I have to get out of here.

He kicked the covers off and rallied his strength. With gritted teeth he slid to the edge of the bed and let his feet fall to the floor.

He coughed. Thick smoke burned his eyes. A light suddenly flickered in the corner of the room. He panicked and the fear made him even more determined.

In one continuous motion he swung his body up and stood. Hundreds of needles seemed to push through his skull at once. He felt his strength, his determination start to fade. His knees began to buckle beneath him.

"Al . . . Al," Moses called to him.

Murphy tried to yell, but the attempt ended in a hacking cough. He took a wobbly step and began to fall. Someone grabbed him.

"I got you, Al," Moses said, gently leading him through the smoke-filled room.

Outside, Murphy gulped the fresh air into his lungs. The intense pain in his head was gone, leaving a dull throbbing. Moses led him alongside the burning building.

Gunshots roared from the street in front of them. Both men sought cover by ducking behind the store.

The shots ended as suddenly as they had erupted. A crashing sound came from the front of the building and Murphy watched ashes and embers float high in the night sky above giant flames.

"The jail . . . Help me to the jail."

Leaning on Moses, Murphy headed down the street. Dressed in long underwear, and keenly aware of every pebble under his tender bare feet, he watched several men running with buckets of water toward the store. It's no use, he thought. They can't save it.

He tightened his arm around Moses and started for the jail. Thirty feet in front of it, two men lay in the dirt. The glow from the fire reflected off the badge on the sheriff's chest. Murphy pointed, and Moses helped him to the man. "Laker," Murphy said, kneeling.

The sheriff turned his head. "It . . . was . . . Gibson," he whispered hoarsely.

Murphy stood up slowly, trying to steady himself as his headache worsened. "Moses, take him to the jail. I can make it alone."

Laker was a big man, but Moses was able to carry him without trouble. Murphy took a step and someone grabbed him around the waist. He looked around. It was Skeet.

Moments later they were in the jail. Moses laid the sheriff on a bunk in the first cell. Murphy sat on the bed with him and looked up at Skeet and Moses. "Go get the other man."

Laker's breathing was harsh and unsteady. Blood covered his shirt. He choked, and foamy blood trickled from the corner of his mouth.

A loud explosion accompanied by a storm of gunshots boomed in the direction of the mercantile, drawing Murphy's attention. The fire, he thought. It's set off the ammunition in the store.

Murphy looked back at Laker. The sheriff moved his hand to his breast, over the star pinned to his shirt. "You have to—to take it." In the same instant, the lawman tore the badge from his shirt. His arm flopped to the side and the badge fell to the floor. He was dead.

Murphy slowly picked up the blood-smeared badge and examined it. *I swore I'd never wear it again—never be forced to do what it requires.*

Skeet and Moses came through the door carrying the other man. "This one's dead," Skeet said. They lowered the body of the man to the floor.

Murphy rose. His strength had left him as suddenly as it had come and he staggered to the man. A deputy sheriff's badge was on the man's chest. Murphy did not recognize him.

Murphy raised his head and saw the lantern-lit room spin around him. He looked down and the plank floor seemed to rise to meet his face. The light in the room swiftly turned dark and he lost consciousness.

# CHAPTER 16

AL MURPHY WOKE. His mouth and throat were dry. He tried to swallow but could not. He searched his surroundings. A square of sunlight was on the dirt floor and he looked at the barred window in the wall above him where the light came through. He shifted his eyes and saw a wall of bars around him.

Bit by bit, thoughts came and he remembered the events of the previous night. He arose and sat on the edge of the cot, holding his throbbing head. He stood and followed the bars with his hands to steady himself until he reached the front office.

Skeet sat in the office. "What do you think you're doin'?"

Murphy tried to speak, but his thick tongue and parched mouth would not permit it. Skeet poured a cup of coffee and handed it to him. The hot liquid helped, but Murphy had his mind on something stronger.

Seeing Laker's desk, he went to it and found a bottle in the second drawer. He uncorked it and drank. The whiskey burned his mouth and throat. He chased the drink with coffee, then dumped half the coffee on the plank floor and filled the cup with whiskey.

"Where's Moses?" Murphy asked, his voice back.

"He's over at the store, searchin' the rubble. They ain't nothin' left of it—or the bunkhouse. Gibson done a good job. I figure he knew you was there."

"Christine?"

"She left with her ranch foreman, Ned, two nights ago. Said she was goin' to the fort to ask for the major's help in gettin' the freight through. Don't much matter now. They ain't no supplies to haul."

Murphy put the cup to his lips. The news about Christine bothered him. Especially the fact that Ned was with her. The whiskey revived him and made him keenly aware of the craving in his belly. "Can you get me something to eat? Some clothes?"

"Done got the clothes." Skeet went to a cot in the corner and picked up a bundle and a pair of boots.

"They're Laker's," he said, putting them on the desk in front of Murphy. "Don't guess they'll fit, but they're better 'n what you got on. His gun's there too."

"Thanks," Murphy replied. "About that food?"

"I can see you're gettin' better. Already orderin' folks around. I'll get you some stew down at the Hash House, but don't go gettin' the idea I'm your maid. No respect for old folks. That's the trouble with you young folks today . . ."

Skeet left the jail. Murphy drank the rest of the coffee-whiskey mixture in one swallow. I guess my clothes, my gun, and my money are gone, lost in the fire.

Things have changed, Mr. Gibson, he thought. Now the fight's coming straight to you.

Hastily Murphy put on Laker's clothes. The shirt and pants were too large, and too short. The boots fit sloppily. They'll do, he thought, strapping on the gun belt. They'll have to.

He carefully examined the dead lawman's Colt .44, wishing he had his Smith. In comparison, the Colt felt cheap and the action rough. "Guess it'll have to do, too." He sighed.

Murphy ejected six hulls from the gun. Laker tried, he thought, until the bullets ran out. I wonder if he hit any of them? Murphy loaded the gun with shells from the cartridge belt. His thoughts turned to that first day, the day he rode the *grulla* toward Turrett. My bullets ran out too, he thought. I might have wound up like Laker.

Murphy felt better, stronger. The whiskey, the clothes, and the gun all contributed to a sense of well-being. He sat back down and took the bottle from the desk. It clanked lightly against something and he set the bottle to the side. Then he saw it.

A badge.

It was smeared with blood and a piece of torn cloth hung from the back. Laker's last words came to him: *You have to—to take it.*

He stared at the badge for several minutes. In it, in the blood, he saw parts of his past. One scene was especially haunting—a boy, maybe seventeen years old, dangling at the end of a rope. The boy kicked and screamed and gagged for what seemed forever before death finally ended his suffering.

And it was for nothing. The boy had killed a young man in a fair fight. Somebody said that the man who had been killed was from a spread out north of town and was the only son of local people. It wasn't true—both cowboys had ridden up with a herd. They were both strangers. The outfit they worked for had busted up and moved on, leaving the two young men to drink their wages up.

The town of Fletcher went mad with it, couldn't live unless they took revenge for the death of "one of it's own." Murphy had tried to stop the hanging. To do the thing required by the badge he wore, but the fine upstanding fools of Fletcher would not listen. One of them hit him with a pick handle from behind and they took the kid and they hanged him and Murphy was helpless to stop it.

The badge. Because of it he had stayed in Fletcher after the lynching and fought Ike Scranton, the father of the boy whom the town had hanged. Scranton and his men came in from Texas and would have destroyed the town and killed everyone who was even remotely connected with

the hanging if Murphy had not stayed. The fight had cost
Murphy. He had taken a bullet in his left arm and leg and
had almost died from the bleeding.

When it was over, a stranger to the town, an English-
men, was the only one who helped him. The only one who
kept Murphy from dying in the dusty street.

Skeet came into the jail, carrying a bowl with cheesecloth
covering it. "I brung you some stew and I saw the doctor
at the Hash House. He asked about you and I told him
you was up and around. He said he'd be here shortly. He
said he wants to change your bandage and talk to you
about somethin'."

Skeet placed the stew on the desk and noticed the badge
in Murphy's hand. "Well?"

"Well, what?"

"Well, ain't you gonna tell me what you're gonna do
with that badge?"

Murphy set the badge down and ignored the question.
The stew smelled delicious and he uncovered the bowl.

"Well?" Skeet asked, sitting on the corner of the desk.

Murphy took a bite without looking at him.

"So this is the thanks I get for gettin' you the clothes
and the food. You won't even talk to me, won't even tell me
what you're gonna do. Just act like I ain't even here. Like
I didn't see you with that badge in your hand."

Murphy looked up and smiled. "I'm going to eat this
stew, Skeet. Thanks for bringing it."

"Well, that cuts it. They ain't no reason for you to treat
me this way. If I was a few years younger, why I'd show
you what-for and . . ."

The door opened and Moses came in, smiling. "I found
it, Al. I sure did find your gun."

Murphy stood up from the desk chair and Moses
handed him the weapon. It was the Smith. The handles
were charred, and it was covered with black soot.

If, Murphy thought, if the fire didn't set the bullets off and if the cylinder will turn, the gun may not be too badly damaged. He broke the gun open. The cylinder moved freely and he ejected the shells. Not one had gone off.

Murphy slapped Moses happily on the back. "Thanks. I missed it more than anything else. Once it's cleaned up, it'll work as good as ever. I'll get some new handles made for it the first time I get a chance."

"Uh—hmmmm," said a short man of indeterminate age with hair that was almost completely gray. He stood in the open doorway, a bag in his hand. It was the doctor, the same man who had cleaned and bandaged his side.

"Come in, Doc," Murphy said, setting the Smith on the desk.

The doctor wasted no time. "Sit down, Mr. Murphy." He set his bag on the desk and took out a pair of scissors. "How's your side?"

"It's about healed up. I guess my head must not be too bad. I'm feeling a lot better."

"Ummm," the doctor said after he had removed the bandage. He took a small mirror from his bag and positioned it so Murphy could see the long furrow on the right side of his skull which extended from his brow to behind his ear.

The sight shocked Murphy. It looked bad, really bad. His hair had been shaved around the wound and the skin that surrounded it was a deep purple.

"A little deeper," the doctor said, "and there is no way you would have lived. Right now, we have to be sure it doesn't become infected. The skin will grow over it, but you'll always have an indention in your skull."

Murphy looked away from the mirror, his thoughts on Gibson. Until now, the man had been nothing more than an enemy. Any enemy. Now, Murphy hated him. As passionately as he had hated the seven men he had killed after Midge's death. "Gibson owes a lot . . ."

"That's something I have been asked to talk to you about," the doctor said, taking a towel and a small bottle from the bag. "Dick Laker told several of us . . ."

"Ouch!"

"I—I forgot to tell you that would burn a little."

"Burn isn't the word for it," Murphy mumbled.

"As I was saying, Dick Laker told several of us on the town's board of trustees about your past law experience. He spoke highly of you and believed you were a man who could be trusted."

The doctor stopped talking and reached in the medical bag again. He took out a round tin of ointment and continued, "I don't think you're well enough, or will be well enough for some time, but the other board members want me to ask if you would be interested in replacing Laker as sheriff of Turrett County."

Murphy did not answer. The doctor put the bottle and ointment back in the bag and took out a roll of bandaging material. He continued to speak while working. "If you were to take the job, which I feel you are in no condition to do, you must set your personal feelings toward Bernard Gibson and Christine McCormick aside and uphold the letter of the law. At this time, the judge has issued an arrest warrant for Gibson."

I don't need it, Murphy thought. Wearing a badge would only complicate matters. Gibson is going to pay for what he has done.

Murphy started to answer, to tell the doctor no, when he thought of Christine. Her absence, and the company she traveled with, worried him. If he wore the badge, he'd have more authority to protect her.

He took the badge from the desk and studied it, then pinned it to his shirt. "I'll take the job."

# CHAPTER 17

AL MURPHY WENT outside and leaned against the south wall of the sheriff's office, rolling a cigarette and relaxing in the early morning sun. Christine should be back today, he thought. She should have already been back.

Two days had passed since he had accepted the job of sheriff. Two quiet days, and he had used them to rest. He wanted to ride to the fort and try to find Christine, but he knew he was too weak to sit a saddle for any length of time.

The town board had given him an advance on his first month's salary, and he had used the money to clean up, shave, and buy a set of clothes—from Gibson's mercantile. There was no other place to get them.

It had been comical. The store clerk was so nervous Murphy had to remind him to ring up the bill. There was no sign of Gibson.

Murphy took a last puff on his cigarette and flicked the butt to the side. I wonder where Gibson is? I can't ride too far, but I might be able to make it to Gibson's ranch. I'll get a horse from the livery. Maybe since he lost his house, he's holed up in a line shack somewhere.

Murphy went into his office to get a rifle, a box of shells, and a canteen. Skeet and Moses both sat by a small wood-stove, grinning. Each had a coffee cup in his hand and a shiny deputy sheriff's badge on his chest.

"Look, boys," Murphy said. "I told you that you could stay here because you had nowhere else to go. But you're not going to be my deputies. I don't need or want deputies. Take those badges off and put them back in the desk."

Moses stood. "Naw, Al. We got no job now, and this is the only way we know to help Miss Christine—and you."

"I don't need any help. Don't need anyone else to worry about. Those badges are nothing more than targets for Gibson and his men. They'll kill you both."

"Maybe," Skeet said, throwing the coffee grounds from his cup onto the floor under the stove. "But they ain't nothin' left for us and it ain't right."

Skeet opened the side door of the woodstove and spit tobacco juice on the coals inside. "Why, I drove the first freight wagon of supplies to the store. I was here from the start. Christine, and Jake too, well, they was real square with me. You're standin' against Gibson—and we got ever bit as much right to be there with you."

Murphy went to the gun rack. I could use their help, he thought. Someone I can trust to stay here at the jail and keep an eye on things. Help Christine when she gets back and watch out for Gibson. I can't be everywhere at once. But . . .

He took a Winchester from the rack and a box of shells from a shelf below. "No," he said. "One or both of you would get killed and I'd feel responsible. I can't risk it."

"Al . . ." Moses' voice was serious, pleading. "You saved my life at the fort. You and Miss Christine and Mr. Skeet treat me good. Better 'n anybody ever done. I want to help. I got to."

"Moses, you don't owe me anything. You saved me too, remember? If you do this, there's a good chance you'll die."

"It be my life. Nobody tell me what I can and can't do with my life—no more."

"Skeet." Murphy turned to him. "They'll kill you if they can."

"Maybe. But both barrels of my Greener is goin' off 'fore they do. I'll give 'em what-for. They won't be forgettin' me."

Murphy went to his desk and set the rifle and shells down. There was a strange feeling in his gut, his chest. It had to do with Skeet, with Moses. He cared; they were his friends. He hadn't allowed himself to be that close to anyone in a very long time.

He searched the desk drawers for a copy of the oath, but was unable to find it.

"Skeet," Murphy said, "get up and stand beside Moses. Both of you raise your right hand."

It was all he could do to say the words, to give what he knew might very well be their death sentence. "Do you both solemnly swear to perform the duties of a peace officer in respect to the laws and—and statutes of the United States of America, Territory of New Mexico, and Turrett County to the best of your ability? Say 'I do.'"

"I do," they said in unison.

"All right," Murphy said. He picked up the rifle and the box of shells.

"Where you goin'?" Skeet asked.

"Out to Gibson's ranch. I'm going to try to look him up. I won't be back until late tonight. You stay here in town and wait for Christine. She should show up sometime today. If she does, you take her out to the ranch and stay with her. Moses can stay in town."

Murphy paused a moment. "Moses—you know how to use a gun?"

"Sure do, a rifle. I learned it in the cavalry."

"Take one of them"—Murphy pointed to the rack—"and load it full. You keep watch on Gibson's store. If he comes in while I'm gone, don't do anything. Just watch and wait until I get back."

"Sure will, I do it just that way."

Murphy started out the door. "Be careful, both of you."

# CHAPTER 18

IT WAS LATE that night before Murphy rode back into Turrett from Gibson's ranch. The forty-mile ride had been fruitless, other than that he had seen several head of Slash M cattle on Gibson's range.

The ride had sapped him of his strength, and now he slumped in the saddle, his head pounding heavily. The sorrel gelding he rode, Laker's horse, automatically turned and stopped at the livery.

Murphy grunted as he stepped from the horse. His legs were stiff, and the muscles between his shoulder blades were sore from hours of holding his body upright. He loosened the latigo to remove the saddle, then he heard a noise and a voice behind him.

"It's me," Skeet whispered.

Murphy turned. "What are you doing up? It must be midnight or after."

"It's closer to two. I been waitin' for you. Moses seen Gibson goin' in the back of his store around eleven-thirty."

Immediately Murphy's nerves tensed and his heart began to beat rapidly.

"There's more," Skeet stepped closer to Murphy. "They's a half a dozen men with him—and, well, they got Christine."

"Christine! Is he sure it was her?"

"He's sure. He was hid behind some empty barrels. They walked by no more 'n a few feet from him."

Murphy's head still throbbed, his legs and back still hurt, but he felt none of it. All of his attention was focused on the news he had received. His mind whirled with questions. How long had they held her? Where had they kept her before bringing her here? Had they killed Ned?

"Get Moses, and both of you meet me back at the jail. Don't light a lamp. If one is already burning, blow it out."

"What're you gonna do?"

"I don't know. But something. We're going to do something."

Murphy unsaddled the sorrel and put him in a corral without knowing he did so. His mind spun with possibilities. Burn them out, he thought. That would be the easiest, except for Christine. They may have her locked up in a room and we couldn't get to her. She might die in the fire.

What then? His thoughts continued. If we bust in and she's being guarded, they'll kill her, or at the least use her for a shield to make their escape. Besides, we won't be able to see in the night. We might shoot each other.

Murphy stepped lightly on the porch boardwalk in front of the jail. I've got to know more, he thought.

Inside, he spoke in a hushed tone. "Skeet? Moses?"

"We here," Moses replied.

Murphy made his way in the darkness to his desk and sat down. "Skeet, do you know the layout of Gibson's place? Where all the rooms are on the first and second floor?"

"Some of 'em. I was only in the top part once, a long time ago, when Gibson tried to get me to go to work for him. His office was at the end of the stairs, first room to the right."

It's not enough, Murphy thought. I need to know the position of every room, and there isn't much time. "Is there anyone in town that would know, that you can trust?"

"They's lots of folks know"—Skeet paused a moment—"but none of 'em I'd trust. They're all hooked up with Gibson."

There was a minute of silence before Murphy spoke again. "We'll have to do it without knowing. We'll—we'll just have to do it."

"Do what?" Skeet asked.

"I don't . . ." An idea came to Murphy and he smiled. "How would you like to play the piano, Skeet? You could serenade the whole town at daybreak."

"You know I can't play nothin'."

"It doesn't matter. You can bang on it, can't you?"

"Yeah, I could pound on it. That one at the saloon plays by itself. Somebody just has to pump the foot pedal. What you figurin' on? A piano ain't gonna do nothin'."

That's even better, Murphy thought without answering Skeet. It would be nice if the noise sounded good.

# CHAPTER 19

THE LIGHT OF dawn was faint in the east when Murphy, Moses, and Skeet took their positions. Skeet hid behind the saloon piano, which now sat in the street—ten feet in front of the entrance to Gibson's Mercantile. Getting it there would have been a real problem, except for Moses.

Moses knelt beside the first-floor rear door, a loaded Henry rifle in his hands. Murphy had climbed the outside stairs in back and knelt on the landing beside a second-floor entrance door. He looked to the east. Will the sun ever come up? We have to be able to see. Be able to see clearly.

A rooster crowed nearby, then another in the distance. The long ride of yesterday in the hot sun with his head injury, plus no sleep and the anticipation of what he was about to do, had worn him to a frazzle. A drink, he thought. How I wish I had a drink.

He looked down and vaguely saw Moses beside the door. It won't be long now, he thought.

Ten minutes later, the piano began to play "Camptown Races." The notes were loud in the morning stillness and dogs in several parts of town began to bark.

Murphy held the Smith in one hand and a sawed-off twelve-gauge in the other. He braced his lanky frame. Not yet, he told himself. Wait, wait for the blast of Skeet's Greener.

The music played on. One minute—two. It seemed forever before it came. Two explosions from the Greener tore the morning apart.

Murphy hit the locked door with his shoulder, using all

the strength and momentum he could muster. It broke loose and two of the window panes in it fell to the floor. A narrow dim hall appeared in front of him and he ran its length to a place where the hall cornered and changed directions.

Gunshots thundered from both the front and back of the store. A man in long underwear, gun in hand, hurried into the hall from a side room. He saw Murphy. Surprise was all over his face. He raised his gun.

Murphy pointed the Smith and pulled the trigger. The man spun a half circle with the impact of the bullet, dropped his gun, and fell.

Footsteps, hollow-sounding on the wood floor, reached Murphy's ears. They were coming from an opening in the hall to his left. He ran to it, stopped, and peered around the corner.

A bullet struck the wall inches above his forehead, and splinters, plaster, and bullet fragments hit his face. He knelt, unable to see, and shifted the shotgun to his right hand. He cocked the right hammer, pointed it around the corner, and fired. The recoil threw his hand back violently and he almost dropped the gun.

Murphy quickly wiped his eyes with his shirt sleeve. His vision returned, but it was blurred. Shots continued to roar below him. He leaped across the opening, pointing the Smith and looking into the space. It was a stairwell and a body lay sprawled three quarters of the way up it.

Murphy flattened himself against the next wall. He saw a movement to the left out of the corner of his eye and swung the Smith around to it.

Too late. He'd seen it too late.

A puff of gun smoke appeared from a partially opened doorway at the end of the hall. Murphy's right leg went out from under him and he fell. When he hit the floor, he dropped the Smith, rolled once, and fired the remaining load of buckshot at the door.

The door was smashed in half and blown open by the shot. Instantly a man appeared in the doorway, a gun in his hand.

Gibson.

Murphy rolled back, searching for the Smith. A shot rang out, and a bullet struck the floor beside Murphy's head. He heard Gibson laugh. Murphy's fingers touched his revolver and another shot came. The bullet hit his right shoulder and knocked his hand away from the Smith.

Again he heard Gibson's laughter.

Two shots fired in quick succession sounded from behind him. He looked back and saw Moses, the Henry rifle at his waist, smoke coming from the end of the muzzle.

Murphy grabbed the Smith and tried to stand. A hazy fog of gun smoke filled the hall. Through it, he saw Gibson's lifeless body curled on the floor.

Moses took Murphy under the armpit with one hand and helped him up. A scream came from a room across from them.

"Christine," Murphy yelled.

There was no sanity left in Murphy. He was wild—completely out of control. He jerked away from Moses and rushed the door. His wounded leg buckled beneath him and he fell, hitting the door with his shoulder at full momentum and banging it open.

A shot was fired from within the room. Murphy slid beside a bed and raised up, looking over the Smith.

Ned!

Christine's foreman had his arm locked around her throat and a gun pointed at her head. "I'll kill her. I swear I will." He backed into a corner. "She'd already be dead except she wouldn't sign the deed. Gibson promised me the McCormick ranch if I helped him. I'm going to . . ."

Murphy did not think. Did not rationalize. Had no idea of his actions or the possible consequences of them. He pulled the trigger on the Smith and the gun jumped in his hand. The bullet went into Ned's head, between his eyes. Drops of blood dotted the wall behind him. Ned jerked backward and his gun flew into the air.

And it was over. In moments, nothing but the sound of Christine's breathing remained. And the smoke with the stench of burnt gunpowder, and the blood.

Murphy used the bed to help himself up. He went to her and held her. Then he staggered and fell.

# CHAPTER 20

"YOU SHOULD A SEE'D that piano," Skeet bragged to Murphy. "They wasn't an inch that didn't have a bullet hole in it and there I was, right behind it, shootin' my Greener and reloadin' just as fast as I could. I got three of 'em, you know. I gave 'em what-for. They won't be forgettin' me."

Christine and Moses came into the small room. "All right, Mr. Al Murphy," she said, smiling. "You've been in bed here at the doctor's office almost three weeks. The doc said we can get you up, if we are very careful. Skeet and Moses and I have something we want to show you."

It took some time, more than a half hour, but at last they had Murphy standing in the main street of Turrett, blindfolded, with a crutch under one arm.

"All right, Skeet," Christine said. "Take the blindfold off."

Murphy blinked in the bright sunlight. He saw his horse, the *grulla*, fat and slick, tied to a hitching rail in front of a building, a new, small building made of rough planks that were so green sap still oozed from them.

He looked up at a large sign.

MCCORMICK—MURPHY—AMES—COFFIN

MERCANTILE

Murphy grinned. "Who's Ames? Coffin?"

"I'm Ames," Skeet said. "Don't you even know who I am? After all we been through and you don't even . . ."

Murphy turned to Moses. "I be Coffin," Moses said, smiling. Then he laughed.

Christine put her arm around Murphy and hugged him. And the odd thing, the thing called fate, still gripped Al Murphy. This time with gentleness and a new beginning.

If you have enjoyed this book and would like to receive details about other Walker Western titles, please write to:

Western Editor
Walker and Company
720 Fifth Avenue
New York, NY 10019